W O O D S M E N

American Indian Literature
and
Critical Studies Series
Gerald Vizenor, General Editor

Woodsmen

O R

THOREAU &

THE INDIANS

A Novel

by Arnold Krupat

University of Oklahoma Press
Norman and London

The lines of poetry on pp. 59, 132, and 133 are from *Pilgrims* by Jean Valentine. Copyright © 1965, 1966, 1967, 1968, 1969, by Jean Valentine. Reprinted with the permission of Farrar, Straus & Giroux, Inc.

PS 3561 .R85 W66 1994

KRUPAT, ARNOLD.

WOODSMEN, OR, THOREAU & THE
INDIANS

n-Publication Data

: a novel / by Arnold Krupat.

:ature and critical studies

....ginally published. New York : Letter Press, 1979. With new pref.
  ISBN 0–8061–2671–X (alk. paper)
    1. Indians of North America—New York (State)—Fiction.
  2. College teachers—New York (State)—Fiction.   3. Land tenure—New York (State)—Fiction.   I. Title.   II. Title: Woodsmen, or, Thoreau and the Indians.   III. Title: Thoreau & the Indians. IV. Title: Thoreau and the Indians.   V. Title: Woodsmen. VI. Series.
PS3561.R86W66   1994
813'.54—dc20   94-12134
                                                             CIP

Woodsmen, or Thoreau & the Indians is Volume 11 in the American Indian Literature and Critical Studies Series.

The paper in this book meets the guidelines for permanence and durability of the Committee on Production Guidelines for Book Longevity of the Council on Library Resources, Inc. ∞

1   2   3   4   5   6   7   8   9   10

"You live in a world of your own Henry."
"I can certainly improve on what was given," Henry said.

DONALD BARTHELME
Snow White

They were a group of that kind of person.

GRACE PALEY
Enormous Changes at the Last Minute

PREFACE

Woodsmen was originally published in 1979 by the Letter Press, a private enterprise undertaken by Cynthia Krupat and me. The story was set in 1976, just after Richard Nixon had resigned the presidency, about the time of the American Bicentennial celebration in July. The upcoming November presidential election offered a dim glow of hope (a little light, as it now appears) before the Reagan-Bush years, the dark night of the American soul.

Inspired by events both personal and political, *Woodsmen* was an attempt to imagine a community "in the American grain" (in William Carlos Williams's phrase), a group of people who tried to live in accord with important, but largely occluded, values in America. Some of these values—such things as nonacquisitiveness, harmony with nature, and commitment to a life of principle—I had increasingly come to identify with Henry David Thoreau, and in the mid-1970s I began to identify these values with the people Thoreau had vaguely named in his last word on earth: "Indian."

The year 1976 was only three years after the occupation of Wounded Knee, South Dakota, by members of the American Indian Movement, an event still remembered warmly by some Native people and deeply regretted by many others. I had seen accounts of the events at Wounded Knee in the newspapers, but, like many Euro-Americans—especially eastern, urban Euro-Americans—I understood little or nothing about what was involved. My schooling in American history had said nothing about the Ghost Dance and the massacre of Big Foot's Minneconjou people on Wounded Knee Creek, nothing about the Dawes Act, the horrors of the boarding schools, or the Termination policy of the 1950s. Indians had been plugged into the national narrative only sporadically and then always in cameo roles as people who had somehow vaguely aided the Pilgrims, defeated George Armstrong Custer, and cinematically circled many a wagon train full of earnest settlers headed west. In much the same way, my instruction in American literature had permitted Native people only a limited or adjunctive visibility: Indians were available as faithful companions to Natty Bumppo or as bedfellows and shipmates to Ishmael. None of my teachers had ever bothered to point out that the "Territory" for which Huck Finn would "light out," was "Indian Territory" — not the "virgin land" of Henry Nash Smith, but soon to be what Francis Jennings called "widowed land."

Only after graduate school did I read William Carlos Williams's *In the American Grain* and D. H. Lawrence's *Studies in Classic American Literature* and discover their belief that it is impossible to understand American history, culture, and literature without first coming to terms with the simple but weighty fact of the indigenous presence on this continent. Native Americans had been *here* for thousands of years; American history had begun long before the coming of the Europeans. It would take a little longer for me to comprehend that the enabling condition for American "civilization" was genocide and that, as Jimmie Durham has written, "The U.S. is a continual and movable holocaust."

When in the 1970s I first began to think about Native Americans, I did so in the way I had thought about everything that intrigued and interested me, by trying to imagine them in a novel. I didn't know then that the narrative mode, storytelling, was central to all Native American cultures, nor did I know, in deciding to narrate my novel in the first-person plural, that Native people traditionally constructed their sense of the self, the "I," in close relation to the tribal or communal "we." *Woodsmen* is the result of my first attempt to think about Native people as central to the narrative of—quoting the Cuban critic, Fernandez Retamar—"our America."

My subsequent attempts to think about Native American history, culture, and especially literature, were carried out analytically—critically, academically, in a meta-narrative manner. Although that kind of work can very easily become a form of colonialism, it can also be put to very different anticolonial purposes, and I remain committed to the critical enterprise. Nonetheless, I know well that you can't think about Native Americans without thinking about and telling stories. And perhaps I will go back to the narrative mode, to telling stories in novels again.

In any case, I am very pleased to have *Woodsmen* issued in the University of Oklahoma Press American Indian Literature and Critical Studies Series, edited by Gerald Vizenor. Although the baby is some fifteen years late, I hope it may yet be welcomed into the world.

Here, I would like to thank Betty Louise Bell for her encouragement and support, not only of *Woodsmen*, but of all my work. My thanks, too, to Pat Hilden, to my son Jeremy, and to my daughter and dear friend, Tanya Krupat. I'm deeply grateful as well to Ralph Salisbury for his warm reception and insightful reading of *Woodsmen*, then and now. A very special word of thanks is due Gerald Vizenor, who for many years has provided friendship and a shrewd critical eye over my shoulder; his willingness to define the American Indian Literature and Critical Studies Series broadly enough to include this book shows an exemplary generosity.

In spite of some temptation, I've made no changes in the 1979 text, and I have also let the original dedication stand. I'd like, however, to dedicate this new edition of *Woodsmen* to Amy Smiley.

New York
January 1994

WOODSMEN

———

When he said he wanted to go to the woods, we said, All right.

The woods were in Walden, he said. Walden, New York. And there was a river. But no pond.

Then he said, My name is Henry.

We paused at that. It was absurd. His name wasn't Henry. We couldn't just say all right.

The radio was on in the other room, the news. For some time now we had been listening to absurdities. And we hadn't once paused. We had just heard the news voice say, Christian gunmen shot down twelve people.

We understood that Christian was intended to distinguish these gunmen from their opponent gunmen who were Moslems, and not to indicate their values. But Christian gunmen, after all: the paradox resounded. But we hadn't paused at that.

So this pause was not very long.

All right, said Hope.

I knew I could count on you, he said. He smiled at us all. Of course I know my name isn't Henry.

His middle name was David, however, though his ancestors had come to America from a Europe far to the East of Thoreau's.

Are you going to buy or rent, said Jules.

No, no, build of course. It wouldn't be right any other way.

Aha! said Jules. And who bankrolls the deal?

It's the material side of moral and esthetic questions that foremost engages Jules who is a Marxist and quite a large person physically. Jules is open and suspicious, a combination of traits not met with all that often. For years he had cheerfully been pointing to bad guys we didn't always see. They were everywhere, he'd said, on our roofs, on our phones, behind parked cars. There, and there, and there.

We'd smiled.

Then when the last President resigned and we heard what he'd been up to, we couldn't help but wonder about our eyes.

So who's your Emerson, Jules said, who supplies the land for this house?

Well, he said, you know, I've got a little money.

We knew he would not have much.

Like the rest of us he earned most of his living working at a profession that paid enough for some comforts but not enough for much of a bank account. Also, he had a wife and two young children.

No one mentioned them. If he was serious, for us to speak of them now might only confuse matters.

Anyway, he said, we bought a little bit of land a couple of years ago when my wife's grandfather died. He left her some money and we thought land was a good thing to have. Land doesn't do war research and this particular little parcel we took out of the hands of the State. We bought it from the State of New York, is what I'm saying. And now I thought I'd like to try and build a little house. Like Thoreau. Live up in the woods for awhile. I can do a lot of the work myself. You all can help me. I know building materials have gone up in price, but think, do you realize how much average life expectancy has increased? On top of everything else this could be a really smart investment.

We knew, both about costs and years. The first we regretted; the second we weren't sure about. People who value high levels of energy and effort are bound to feel guilty about living too long, as if longevity were a sign of miserliness, that we'd selfishly held back. There was also some fear attached. If the body holds up, if the brain can grab enough oxygen, extra years give extra time for work. But what if the brain's no grabber and the body betrays? Our time offered lots of sad illustration of the literal fate worse than death.

Two pails a paint an a brush, said Hope, that's about all you can get now for the amount of money it took Thoreau to build his whole house.

Come on, Hope, he said, really, you're exaggerating.

And we all began to talk at once.

Wait, said Anna, just wait a minute now.

We had mostly been disagreeing about what figure Thoreau had actually given as his cost to build the house he had lived in at Walden.

Why not get a copy of his book, Anna said. Let's at least know what we're talking about.

Yes, said Ariel, O yes!

She had seemed to be staring at the wall all this time, her own quiet place around her, smoke rising from her lips. Now she stubbed out her cigarette, stared hard from one to the other of us, and said, Please, let's do, let's get the *text*. And then, don't you think we could go out*side*?

ℰ

If you will go to the woods like Thoreau, said Hassan, will you also go to prison like him?

This both began and ended a second conversation on the subject.

He did not answer but clearly he would think about it.

So would we all.

We thought about it whenever Hassan was around even if he said nothing. He was a native of that part of the world where the Christian and Moslem gunmen shot each other, though it was not his own country. His own country was run by those whom the CIA had bloodily installed some twenty years ago and presently sustained. They had three times imprisoned Hassan and once tortured him.

We had been through nothing quite like that. But most of us had also gone to prison, at the very least for a day like Thoreau. For committing acts of principle. Hassan had gone for committing poetry. Now that he had come to America and joined our Faculty he was no longer in danger of prison.

Only his life was in danger here.

Jules had told us at length of the various possibilities, which agents of which agencies, ours and theirs, might try to do Hassan in. And how. And when.

I have never been to that part of New York State where this Walden is, said Hassan. Why don't we go? You must show us my friend.

He did not especially fancy the image of himself as tour-guide even for his friends. But taking Hassan's words as a test of his seriousness, he said, Fine, whose car?

If you want to show them, his wife said, Why, you go right ahead and show them. They're your friends, not mine. Show them, if you want to. I'm staying home.

She didn't want to go to the woods to live. Not at all. Things were hard enough even with the vital City for support, the wide wide world, whoever might call or come by or pass through the big town. Tending the kids, trying to get a little work done, cooking cleaning as often as she could, she felt locked in enough without volunteering for the tighter melodrama of The Wilderness Wife. She'd read of that gal, dead now and lucky so, gone mad or gone cold of drudgery and loneliness and firing babies yearly against the green void. For she knew those fine trees did not speak back when spoken to; the white snow was clean and pure and also blank. Would there be any one who read a book for miles around? how many eyes would look further than the monotone green of the neat backyard? She didn't want the woods at all.

Neither did the children. Or, rather, the son thought it might be all right. He had a vision of chainsaws and axes, lots of rope and rigging, maybe some gas-powered version of Babe the Blue Ox. Vroom vroom timber, and such. But the daughter who was older and took ballet lessons supposed quite rightly that these would not be readily available nor much valued in her father's stupid old woods. She had anyhow developed already a habit of siding with her mother when sides were to be taken although she looked a lot like her father. And the mother was adamant: she'd agreed to the purchase of the land, but for now, no woods. Not even a ride up for a look.

This particular marriage had already outlasted most of the others we knew or had made. It was not hard to imagine it was ripe for destruction. Things fell apart as the rule rather than the exception, these days. Emotional, moral, political irresponsibility roared from the loudspeakers as the ideal rather than its shortfall. Still, genuine connection of a deep kind was between our friend and his wife. Anyone giving or taking odds on the future of this union would be wise to take that into account.

We knew how he felt about it, though ignorant of her side. However unfashionable it might be these days for men who thought of themselves as strong and sexy (he did, holding in his tum, think, now and again, of himself as strong and sexy) to like being married, he liked being married. To his wife.

But he would not be done out of his woods.

We didn't know her as well as we did him. She was right, we were his friends. But we thoroughly regretted not knowing her better, however we recognized it as the usual case.

It's always with trepidation that we meet the spouse or lover of one whom we esteem. What if that person seems somehow wrong or not good enough for our valued friend? But when that happens, we never seem to blame our friend for poor judgment but the partner for presumption. How dare such a person establish relation with a being so clearly superior! There seems very nearly something unscrupulous about such an alliance. And it is always the one we knew first whom we take to be the victim.

This couple presented something more complicated than the usual case, for there was not one of us who didn't admire and respect our friend's wife. She and he made a real couple; there was no victim to be labelled in this marriage. Still, when it came to true concern, when it came to loyalty, she was right: he, not she, was our friend.

Hope and Ariel concurred, though reluctantly. And Anna said, Sisterhood is powerful but a friend's a friend.

č

We drove up the Palisades Parkway, on to Route 9W, to Route 52, and then 208, which took us to Walden. Walden, New York.

The station wagon in the lead, with the VW bus following, both machines filled with craggy, cheerful people and backpacks, made us nostalgic, each and severally, for the 'sixties. Bus and wagon passed and re-passed, waves and smiles. And we made a piss stop at an Exxon station, an island with facilities, between two swift streams of traffic.

Everybody came out happy. It was like going down to Washington in '63 for Civil Rights, or for Peace in '65 and '66, right up to '67, after which the mood was different. Good weather then, too, for the good causes, a sense of community and common purpose. A belief, then, that something could be done.

Progressives, said Hope, are people who make sandwiches for lunch that they eat right after breakfast.

Hope had once given an interview in which she had said, People who want to be good interest me.

Not people who want to do good. People who want to be good, a much harder thing.

Ever since God went and cursed all Nature for Man's sin in the Garden, people who want to be good have found themselves at odds with their world. It seems awfully an over-reaction on God's part to have taken any single human mis-step as all that big a deal, but there it is. In a bad world, people who want to be good are always in opposition.

It takes a lot of energy. It gives you an appetite.

č

There was not a pond. But the river he had named, the Wallkill, was in regular view.

It does not seem a river much good for lazy drifting, said Anna. I think of the young Henry Thoreau and his brother and their week on the river.

Anna's voice is beautiful, full and deep. She speaks with just a trace of German accent, the kind that evokes Marlene Dietrich, not the vaudeville comic. Anna says things slowly most of the time and it is rare that even her most casual words don't seem to have a real weight to them.

Before he kept his diary of the woods, Thoreau kept a diary of the waters, a patchwork record of a week he and his older brother John had spent on the Concord and Merrimack Rivers. He early got in the habit of thinking journeys needed their journals. And he paid himself to have this first one published.

Well, said Jules, it does look like a good river for growing onions.

From the first page, second section of the *New York Times* Jules knew about the town of Florida (New York) along the Wallkill where conditions were supposed to be ideal for onions. Jules believed in onions, though he had raised the possibility that the article was actually talking about something else. Everything is a code, Jules often said.

Ariel said, I think it's just lovely. What undramatic water, look at the modest color.

Cold, said Hope, it's just cold.

Children, Ariel said, if we let them, would wade out.

Enough, said Jules, well and good, whatever you say. But I am hungry. And I would like a drink.

No drinking, he said. And, Ariel, if you possibly could, would you try not to smoke?

Trying not to smoke was one of Ariel's chief occupations. At present, she was between tries. Just the week before she had finally admitted flunking a five-week course that had guaranteed she would stop smoking on a designated day. She had stopped—and forty-eight painful hours later had begun again. She'd been puffing quietly away all the ride long.

We can pull in some place for beers later, he said. And, Ariel, you can smoke on the way back. Just not now. Please? If you know what I mean.

Here we are, he said.

And the wagon and the bus pulled into a clearing among some scraggly woods, locust and maple and chokecherry.

We piled out of the machines, stretched, and took deep and meaningful breaths of the clean air. Which did not disappoint. We walked about, a few strong steps in one direction, then another. Here we were in the country! We wanted to be worthy.

Jules pointed to a tree on his right. There was nailed a sign that read

PROPERTY OF

THE POQUOSSET TRIBE.

And then we noticed on a tree to the left was nailed another sign

PROPERTY OF

CONIGLIO BROS., INC.

Where is your sign, said Hassan.

Something's wrong, he said.

I like it, Anna said. Really, it's awfully nice here. So innocent, so American.

Something's wrong, he said. Those trees are mine.

Have you got the deed, Hope said. Where's your deed? Get out the title, right, Jules?

Hope owned a house in Vermont; Jules had a summer cottage on Cape Cod. We breathed easier. Hope and Jules knew about these things.

He had his deed. We examined it together, figuring east and west by the position of the sun which we checked by consulting our watches. The trees seemed well within the acre and a half the official paper said was his.

I better check this out, he said.

While he sat making personal calls from his office phone, a savings in money at a cost in guilt, Ariel's third book of poems came out and Hope and Jules appeared on the *Times*'s OP/ED page on successive days.

He was glad for his friends though it all put him in rueful mind of how much time he had spent changing diapers, doing dishes, remodelling their dilapidated floor-of-a-brownstone.

Enmired in the private detail, cut off from the public existence: something like that was the tendency of his regret.

His friends both male and female also had kids and did chores with no more money than he to place between themselves and the shitwork of the world and still they had succeeded in bringing their work to wider notice. So he could not blame his anonymity entirely on his situation.

They had more talent, probably. But it wasn't only that. More desire, then? and ferocity? spirit for the battle, rage for the race to the fore? More concentration, surely, the ability to exclude and focus when it counted. For all their names were known to more than a small circle of friends.

Not his.

Not *yet*, we corrected, assuring him in honesty not only friendship that his work too would be known, his name familiar to the same few for whom the rest of us publicly existed. If, that is, that was what he wanted. After all, we said, he was still young, a mere child as such things went, just past thirty. (Thirty-*five*, he said, halfway to forty, two toes in the grave!)

He was still young, we said, by several years the youngest of us. We'd read what he'd written, we'd seen how he taught. Never mind great: good, certainly, it was. That wasn't negligible, we said, it was far too early to despond. The world would know his name in time.

Thanks, he said, but forgive me if I don't hold my breath.

Apparently we had not been of any help.

And he reproached himself (as he talked to the man at the bank who'd handled the mortgage, the lawyer who'd presided at the closing, the clerk at the County Hall of Records who'd stamped the official seal to his title) for wasting yet more of the time he needed for the work that would place him in the world on stupid private details. On absurdities, on trivialities.

It's ridiculous, he said. Thoreau never had to deal with all this crap. I should just sell the damn land and forget the whole thing.

Of course he should, we said. If that was how he felt, he should just sell.

This also did not help. In fact, we could see it hurt. Our calm reasonableness was an affront to his impassioned frustration.

Never mind, he said. Never mind. But, damn it, you'll see, I'm going to the woods.

Tony Coniglio was much taller than his brother Joey who was probably near twice his age. Tony had his Honorable Discharge dated 1971 in a frame on the wall of the trailer. As soon as he'd left Viet Nam he'd started right in working for Joey. Bang bang bang, Tony said. Same kind of work, demolition and construction. Of course, no one got killed here. Or hardly ever.

Oh, he said, yes, I see.

It was a nice trailer, warm, comfortable more than we would have thought for a portable office.

They're usually pretty comfortable, Jules said. You can't be a boss if you don't feel entitled to your comfort.

Jules had done strike support work at several construction sites. He had experience.

Joey and Tony were the Coniglio Bros. They had put
up their sign because they knew he was going to sell.
Joey planned to get to work in a couple of months. He
would start on Tony's birthday, a present to his little
brother.

Hey, just wait a minute, he said. Your sign's on my tree.
That's my property, not yours, and I don't want to sell.

Look, said Joey, don't worry. Relax, no sweat, you'll
sell. I can cut ya the tree down if ya like it so much.
I'll cut it up in pieces or in boards or however ya want.
I'll cut ya up a dozen trees if ya want. Hey, you look
like the kinda guy got a woodburnin fireplace, am I
right? I hear they get a hunnerd an a quarter a cord for
firewood down in the City. I'll cut ya up three cords, an
I'll even let ya stack em back a my garage. Look,
waddaya want from a guy?

An that don mean Joey's gonna give ya a penny less for
the land, right Joey? I mean, we ain't that kinda guy.

Absolute. Twelve grand. Ya unnerstan what I'm sayin?
Twelve big ones for a lousy acre an a half a nothin. An
what else, listen, if ya think you're gonna get screwed
what if I find oil or somethin, I'll write it in in the closing
agreement. Oil, uranium, free pussy, whatever. If I find
it, it's yours.

We jus want the lousy parcel, man, said Tony. I'm tellin
ya straight, pal. We're contractors, developers, we ain't
con artists.

c

Behind the other tree, in a manner of speaking, was John Whitlock, Chief of the Poquosset tribe. He was making no offers.

I nailed up that sign, he said, because the land is ours. That tree is on the hereditary territory of the Poquosset. The State had no right to sell you that land because it did not belong to the State. Their title is and has been defective for years. But because my people were scattered, weak and ignorant of their rights, nothing was ever done. Now we are no longer so ignorant and we shall no longer be weak. I assure you of my sincere regret for any inconvenience or financial hardship this matter may cause you. Like many a whiteman before you, you probably blundered into something you knew nothing about. In a spirit of forgiveness and friendship, I would pay you for the land if I possibly could. But I have no particular resources of my own and my people are very poor. Furthermore, whatever little money we can obtain will almost surely have to go to pay court costs. For, though it will help enormously if you cede us the land to which you now have title, the matter does not end with you. What with the State and those gangster developers, we will have plenty to pay the courts. And our only assistance may come from the Native American Rights Fund.

That's a fine organization, he said. I've sent them whatever I could for years.

On the Wednesday afternoon before Christmas his daughter's ballet group was having an open class. Parents and friends were invited to watch the children dance. His daughter's affections were not so detached from him that she didn't want him to come. That same Wednesday afternoon Joey Coniglio had told him to be at Renzo's Bar on Thompson Street. Joey hadn't asked him. He had told him. And he actually had said it was important for his health.

By Tuesday afternoon he had not yet decided what to do. He sat in his office staring out the window. He was waiting for his best student to arrive. This beautiful nineteen-year-old had a crush on him. There was nothing personal in it. Anyone who'd been teaching for awhile would have to understand that. The student-teacher relationship is inherently passionate. Transferring the literary inheritance to the next generation text by text is highly charged business, full of power and light. Good teaching could be a demonstration of potency. And real potency these days could not fail to have its attractions.

He understood this although understanding did not fully confer protection. He saw that she often looked at him when they went over a poem together, not at the important thing, the words on the page.

There had been, there would be, nothing between them but the page. That was too bad perhaps. She was very lovely and he saw it clearly. But it was wiser to let her affection as it presently stood suffice. He would be satisfied, nor would his satisfaction be spoiled because it was his profession more than his person that moved her.

She had called and asked to come by at three-thirty. It was already three-forty. At her last conference she had awkwardly called him by his first name, dropping the Mister she had used all semester long. He looked forward to seeing her. There might be some small pleasure to be taken from principled renunciation. Though tempted to indulge himself, he would not touch her cheek. He would not take her in his arms. And he knew why.

You need a little girl, his wife had several times said. Only half in jest, she had more than once (in despair of her fatigue and short temper, the inevitable curse on the good parent to young children) suggested that he bed an occasional coed. It would be, she had said, only medicinal.

He agreed, only half in jest. I should, he said.

But he didn't. Some desires can't be assuaged by substitute satisfactions. He wasn't exactly sick. So there was no point to medicine.

Almost four o'clock and she still hadn't arrived. Then he saw her outside on one of the College walks in the arms of a young man. They were elaborately kissing just beneath his office window.

This is for my benefit, he understood, to punish me. For

disappointing her. Not, of course, by anything he had done but by everything he had failed to do.

He recognized sins of omission as his particular line of error. Not wrong-acting so much as refraining from action, that was the mistake his sort was prone to.

She had made her point tellingly. He'd known there was a decision to be made and, indeed, he had made one. But from her point of view he'd only evaded. What he meant as difficult renunciation, she had taken as mere cowardice. Or, at best, a poor choice.

The miserable confusion her impending arrival had allowed him to hold off descended with a vengeance. Now he indulged: all the decisions in his path seemed of this sort, damned one way or the other; whatever he did, however he decided, he was screwed. This way or that, someone was mad at him.

He paced about his office. Then he pulled down the window shade. He went to his phone and dialed Hassan's extension.

Will you come have a drink with me, he said.

Hassan did not drink but said yes. A poet should know when to take the literal as metaphor.

Only metaphorically, or with the widest latitude, could his present situation—knowing what to do and fearing the consequences—be compared to Hassan's in Iran. Still, in his small way, Joey Coniglio was as much the terrorist as the CIA thugs who had tortured his friend. In this particular instance, twelve grand was the carrot; a broken nose was the stick.

He had for a long time wanted to speak to Hassan about his experience. There seemed no more important thing to speak about. For prison and pain had come increasingly to be the central tests of our time. Those who endured them, if they survived, lived among us surrounded by a dark glow, a bloody aura of honor peculiar to those who had paid in the flesh for the daring of their minds.

What was it like, he said, when they—When you—

Ah, said Hassan, I see. Well, you are not the first to ask. And everyone of our friends who has asked was a little drunk, or at the least furtive. As if they were seeking out the man who sells dirty pictures on the Place Pigalle. Believe me, I am not making fun. What you want to know, after all, is an obscenity.

I will tell you, as far as I am able. You will see that I was not so brave as you may have imagined, no braver than you would be. Nor was I better prepared for what I had to endure than you would be, or than anyone. One is never prepared for such things. One should not be.

But you did not betray your friends, he said. We know that. You did not tell them what they wanted to know.

True, I did not. But let me assure you that was perhaps

no more than an accident. Immediately after my arrest they began to jeer and mock at me and insult my family. That was unpleasant, but I found I could withstand it easily enough. Then they began to beat me. I suffered, to be sure, but once again, I had not much trouble to withstand. So eventually they became more elaborate. You have probably read the details. They have been published so the world will know. You understand, it is not easy for me to talk of them.

Well, very soon, I was quite ready to speak. I was about to cry out for them to stop. I was about to tell them whatever I knew and to invent what I did not know, just so they would stop. But before I could do that occurred the lucky accident I spoke of. For suddenly it was as if I split into two people. One part of me remained in their hands and tried to scream out, Stop! I will speak! But that other part actually took up a position across the way in that basement room where this business is transacted and literally shook its head in wry amusement at the idiocy of such doings. The part of me that remained in their hands lost consciousness again and again (so, you see, there was pain they inflicted that I did not feel), but that other part kept up its strong ironic vigil. I had no control over it. *It* simply refused to cooperate. I don't know what would have happened had I not soon passed out so that they could not directly revive me.

But let me tell you, my friend, when at last I regained consciousness in my cell, I was quite certain that I had told them all they had asked. For a time, until I was released, I suffered not only from my body's many wounds, but from my firm conviction that I had *not* withstood them, that I had betrayed my friends.

No one can possibly be sure he will withstand. The torturers have always more energy and ingenuity than a decent man could imagine. And nonetheless, some of us do not betray, however it may come about. I have no advice for you, you see. But now you know what I have told other of our friends.

❦

After lunch on Wednesday he called Renzo's Bar and left a message for Joey Coniglio with Angie the barman.

Tell Joey I can't make it, he said. Tell him I won't be able to come meet him this afternoon.

Then he drove into the City to watch his daughter dance.

❦

It was her concentration made her beautiful. Not the many proud parents in the room nor the clutter of the long table set with juices and cakes distracted her. All of herself, the father in wonder saw, she focused on the movements of the dance.

Her concentration made her beautiful but always she was beautiful. How had she got such a wonderfully formed little body with his skewed luck? Not pudgy, not gawky, legs and torso, feet and hands all in perfect proportion: so he saw her. It was not a parent's bias: so she was. The dark hair, the dark eyes were from him. From whom the energy for life in her look? From her mother of course, whom he loved.

The piano stopped. The old woman playing smiled at the dancers, at the audience. The children bowed and held the room in stillness for a moment. Then with other fathers and mothers he and his wife shuffled feet and applauded.

He tried to focus all of himself on the little girl in black leotard and pink tights coming toward him. Yet he could not help his thought's flight to Renzo's Bar, to Joey, to Hassan, to his wife on her feet beside him.

But how much she looked like him! that beautiful concentrated child.

ċ

He makes me feel alive, his wife said. I don't see why you should be so surprised. You know what it's been like lately. You want to go to your woods? O.K., this is my woods.

She had a lover.

She had told him only now that the likelihood became too obvious to bother lying. She hadn't hidden it to spare his feelings. His feelings now and for some time were not of interest to her.

It's a mistake, he said.

Ha! she said. And what have we been doing the last I-don't-know-how-many months? Getting things right? You do your work, you see your friends, you fill your time with this house-in-the-country business. Fine. What's there in it for me? When I cry, when I feel the deadness coming over me, you *explain* to me what's wrong. You cover everything. You get it worked out just right. You start from certain premises and you proceed logically to certain conclusions. Unanswerable, no loopholes. You've got your logic, your—your premises and conclusions, keep them. He wants *me*. He *sees* me. Not like you. At least I can feel something with him. You don't really care anyway.

I care, he said. I'm sorry. I also need. And I care, he said.

č

I didn't know she hated me so much, he said.

We said nothing.

It's not like my woods at all, he said.

Perhaps, if you think, it is, said Anna.

Marriage makes strange bedfellows, Hope said.

Who gets the kids, said Jules, who gets the station wagon?

It may be for the best, Ariel said. Or, you know, maybe it's only a temporary thing. She just may need some room for herself now.

Ariel had married the same man three times. This last divorce, she promised, was it. She knew about temporary.

Yes, said Anna, Ariel may be right. Perhaps it may be for the best. Better for you this way as well as better for her.

Anna more than any of us might say that. She had separated from her husband many years before. She had raised her son by herself and it had turned out well. Handsome, strong, bright, this boy gave hope to us all.

Perhaps it is for the best this way, said Hassan. But I am not the one to tell you so. I miss my wife whom I can so rarely see and I miss and fear for my children.

Yes, yes, he said, that's right. Me, too. They need me, my children. She needs me.

She does not think she needs you, said Anna. You must not falsify and you must not indulge yourself.

Well, she does need me, he said. And anyway, I need her.

That, said Hope, is another kettle of fish.

č

Joey Coniglio, unannounced, turned up, one afternoon, at his office door.

Hey, perfesser, said Joey, poking his head into a discussion of Self and Alienation in the Western World, can ya do me a favor an ditch the doll?

He apologized to the doll, a freshman child but finely made, and asked if she could come back tomorrow. Not the Self, surely not Alienation or the Western World would disappear by then.

So waddaya say, said Joey, so how ya been? I foun out where ya worked easy enough, perfesser. I been checkin ya out. Yeah, yeah. An I give it to ya, ya got balls, you're a pretty classy guy. See, when I first met ya, I didn't know what to think, ya know. I figured ya must be stupid or somethin. Why would a guy take chances, ya know, like when I tol ya to show up an ya didn't show up? Ya do like that, ya got nothin to gain an a lot to lose. So what gives, I ask myself.

An then, like I say, I start checkin, ya know. An I see, degrees, a college perfesser. Ya can't jus plain be stupid. An I give it to ya, yeah. I can unnerstan a guy who don just grab at the first thing comes along. I foun out how much ya make, perfesser. I checked it out, like I say. So then I see, what you get, shit, why shouldn't ya hol out? How many chances is a guy like you gonna get to pick up a piece a change, am I right?

Anyhow, so like ya see, I put myself out an here I am.

I come up here to see you, I don hol no grudges or nothin. Joey Coniglio ain't no slob. I don got no degrees, but I got class, too, perfesser. An, awright, so look, I tol ya I'd give ya twelve? awright, forget the twelve balloons, I'll give ya fifteen. How's that, huh? Waddaya say? Oh, an, forget what I said about your health, O.K.? What I wanna go an break your legs for?

So, O.K., perfesser, now we unnerstan each other a little better, right? Good. I won't rush ya, take your time makin up your mind. On'y hurry up, ya know, me an Tony, we're stuck like this, waitin on you. Gimme a call at Renzo's, O.K.? An do it quick. Me an Tony, I don think we'll be makin any more offers.

❦

It was about this time that the Country began to have an Election for President. It did this every four years and we'd been through it several times before. But this time it took us by surprise.

Maybe that was because, the last two of these Elections having been won by a man of unsurpassing badness, we thought America would just give up on the whole electing-for-President business. If two hundred years of it had led to no better than the creature who had just been forced to resign, maybe common decency would require trying something else.

Of course if we had thought that, it was foolish to believe it. We knew common decency was not a factor when it came to important decisions. What country had ever been governed by a concern for common decency. Still, it felt especially strange, this time, to find another Election getting under way.

It was about this time too that the Country began to prepare its Two-Hundredth Birthday Party. Much was promised for the glorious Fourth of July, sights and sounds, a great profusion of special good and services. We had our freedom. It was our inalienable right to choose freely between Revolutionary Coke and Bicentennial Pepsi. It could not be truly American to celebrate without an orgy of consumption and a hefty profit.

We tried not to be discouraged. It's our country too and there's plenty to be proud of. But it was hard just then to be decently encouraged when all the history dripping from official lips was arrogant and self-serving, when the pageantry was promotional, and everything was for selling.

There was a song we heard everywhere. It went

> *We must be doin something right*
> *To last two hundred years.*

We would hear it through to July and perhaps ever after. But we tried to be encouraged. The Bicentennial of our Country was important to us, too, who felt ourselves very much Americans. And, right or wrong, these days were what the future would call history.

č

On July fifth, 1876, John Whitlock said, stories about America's Centennial celebrations shared space on the front pages of the newspapers with the continuing story of Custer's defeat on the Little Big Horn.

I didn't know that, he said.

Yes, the Chief said. It was the last fight we won. Now, some of my people want to organize a celebration of our own for this July fourth, for your Bicentennial. It would be a Centennial for us, of course, and the date actually to be commemorated would be June twenty-fifth, the day Custer and his war criminals went down. It would be fitting for such a celebration to take place on our hereditary lands.

Oh, he said, I see what you mean.

Yes, said the Chief, I hope you do. Remember, to some extent we depend on you, whether this intention of ours, and other, more long term intentions, can be carried out. Because we were a pre-technological people, a primitive people—or, as some of your young people think, because we were a singularly wise and advanced people, the spirit of place informs our sense of things at every point. The rocks on the land you mistakenly bought, the trees, the special quality of the light at any moment of the day, these are important factors in what we think, what we do, who we are, how we heal and pray. Some of us surviving Poquosset want to live as Indians. It's not a question of turning back the clock. You can't do that, of course. I don't even know for sure what we'll do on this land, once we get it. But what's certain is that's where we have to start, with our land. So, sorry as I am, that's where it's at. It isn't your land, whatever the title says. It can't be.

Have you read Thoreau, he said.

Some, the usual things. Why do you ask.

Nothing, no reason. I was just thinking that the house he lived in at Walden Pond wasn't on his land either. He never owned it. But he made it his, in a sense anyway, by the life he lived there, by the use of it.

Ah. And your name, then, is Henry?

No, no, I know it's not. I wasn't really making a comparison, just thinking. But, look, tell me, you say Custer was a real monster?

Oh, just an American military man, you know. In the great tradition of Sherman and Chivington and Westmoreland. I can lend you some books if you think you're interested.

He moved out. Someone had to. His wife wanted to keep the kids with her. She couldn't trust her babies with him in an alien environment.

But I'm not going to the woods yet, he said. I don't even

know if I ever will. There's some dispute about who owns what. And there's no place to live up there. I couldn't go now even if I wanted to. You're the one who's not happy here. You found somebody else. You move out.

But soon he gave in.

It turned out to be a point against him that he had not taken any step in reaction against the misery she insisted they had been living.

He had often been unhappy. He had seen she often was not happy. Certainly these were hard years. But he had thought things would work out.

Ha, she said, like magic, hmm? Just suddenly get better, just like that?

To which he had no answer.

And if she was staying, and she was, she would also keep the kids.

They need their mother, she said.

Their father, too, he said.

Yeah, she said. But less.

So, she said, that's settled. We stay, you go. You can see the kids weekends, and, really, whenever you want, if you let me know in advance and we can work it out.

He said nothing. He nodded.

And growled as he left. And slammed the door. And cried in the streets.

č

All right, we said, what do you expect. There just is no American precedent for wife and woods together.

He sighed.

He had wanted both. But where was his model?

American precedent said, Live free and uncommitted. Don't let em tie you down. When you can see the smoke from another man's chimney, that's the time to move along. Elbow room said Dan'l Boone. Climb on the raft with Huck, drift on down the River, light out for the territories. Don't let the women hold you, don't let them civilize you. That civilizing, it takes your manhood.

Keep wild, keep free. Watch out for Aunt Sally, hide out from Momma and the Missus.

Neither a dependent child nor a depended-upon parent be: that was the commandment of American precedent. A true son of the Revolutionary Fathers, the Founders, is ready to take off at a moment's notice. The Free-born American Youth is beholden to no one. And can't no one hold him. Spare your tears, Mother, I must be off. Up yours, Wife, I'm headin down the line.

We got the room, we got the power. There's no time a man can't make a new start. Maybe we did weep when we reached the Pacific, land's end. But not even God could close the Frontier on us. When we ran out of continent to conquer, we set out to conquer the world. We finished the Red Man at Wounded Knee but we didn't sit around and mope. By then we'd built the ships (we were hard at work on the planes) so we could stick it to the Yellow. We opened up Japan and China; Korea and Viet Nam were only logical after that. Ain't no way to hold us down. Southeast Asia today and tomorrow the moon. Or yesterday, already. And even the moon's a stepping stone.

The American boy is always the new-man. Metamorphosis is in the American grain, perpetual change, not fixity, not commitment. Commitment cuts down on infinite possibility, narrows free choice. And what kind of freedom do you call that? Maturity, you call it? But that's a joke. There's no excitement in what's settled. Beginnings, that's what we want, the new! the new! And stay forever young. Better not to talk of the middle: middle-life, middle-road, middle-class. We are it, we have it, but damned if we'll acknowledge it. Admit the middle and the next thing you know there's the unspeakable end.

In these regards, we said, even your beloved Thoreau was a typical American. He advised that we live free and uncommitted for as long as possible. The central part of him is the Poet of eternal beginnings. His work is full of the imagery of dawn and morning.

And remember Thoreau never married, we said, he never

had children. He went to the woods alone. Not even Thoreau could manage to have woods and wife at once.

But our friend still wanted both.

Whatever American precedent might urge, wholeness was his goal, what he meant by wife and woods. It was intolerable to think of beauty unconjoined with utility, of success as never wedded to decency. Even in our world, couldn't jack work many trades and still be clear master of one? There had to be a way for life's million pieces to be integral, not separate strands of clashing colors but fabric of all, whole cloth. He thought of the circle and the spectrum, not the ladder, a world where value was inherent in the very fact of existence, not a function of placement, high or low. On *that* ground one could build, make judgments and fine discriminations, try hard to be good.

All that stuff's in Thoreau, too, he said, who learned it nowhere but from Nature.

Fine, we said, admirable. It's in what Indians believe as well. But you're an American and who are you to swim against two hundred years? Face it, in America there's just no way to have what you want, to have both wife and woods.

Bullshit, he said, a lot you know.

And so when he said he wanted to go to the woods, we had to say, All right.

I don't want to go alone, he said. Of course, I could take the kids.

He paused.

But I don't think I should take the kids. And I don't want to go alone.

We said, All right.

The radio was on in the other room. The news voice informed us that fallout from a Chinese bomb was on its way to New York and Pennsylvania. The cows would eat death in the grass. We were to be careful of our milk. A Cuban plane had been blown up over the Caribbean. No survivors. In Northern Ireland gunmen had shot three women and two children in retaliation for the shooting of two women and three children. The gunmen on both sides this time were Christian.

Child abuse was on the rise. There was a number to call if you heard children screaming. Studies showed that Channel 7 had the most violence of the three major networks. Channel 7 had just taken the lead in the ratings from Channels 2 and 4. There was no number to call if you heard the television screaming.

We would go to the woods.

č

Large blocks of ice floated in the river. Except for the road the ground was white. We went through Walden and stopped in his woods.

There was a large tent pitched among the trees. A thin curl of smoke rose above the peak.

Smell! said Ariel, how sweet! They're burning apple wood. Doesn't it smell good!

It smells great, said Hope, if you can smell. You sit around in one of those, you get a cold in the nose for sure.

I'm going back to the bus for an extra sweater, Jules said, wait up for me a minute.

We approached the entrance flap of the tent. It seemed ridiculous to knock.

He pulled open the flap, stooped, and went in. We followed.

John Whitlock sat on a mattress pointing a shotgun at us. On either side of him sat a woman, each with a rifle in her hands.

Ah, it is you, said the Chief lowering his weapon, welcome. As one of your distinguished poets wrote, One cannot be too careful these days. Let me present my sister, Jane Fawn Coat. And on my left, here, this is our friend, Maria deFrise. Won't you sit down? There are some more mattresses over there, and some blankets if you're cold.

What's going on, he said. You didn't tell me about this.

No, you're right. Sorry. But when I had no word from you as to your plans, and then when we started getting some threats from those gangsters who call themselves developers, all the while various other members of our tribe were arriving, well, something had to be done, even if it was only symbolic. So we set up this tent on the land. Symbols are important to us, anyway.

And here you are in your canvas wigwam catching pneumonia, said Hope.

Only a slight cold, so far, John said. But listen, my friend, we're waiting. What have you decided?

I need this land even more than before, he said. A lot of things have changed for me. I can't live at home any more, and, I tell you, the developers have threatened me too and I'm scared. So I don't know what to do, John. I just think I really need to talk to you. I guess I need your help to know what to do.

O.K., the Chief said, all right. Even the Lone Ranger couldn't make it without Tonto. Why shouldn't you have your faithful Indian companion too?

č

So our woods-wanting friend also entered for a time into the archetypal American alliance. Man and wife have never formed our model couple. For us it's always been two males for the woods, for the road, or the waters. Two males, not quite equals; usually, one white, one not, Paleface and Indian—red or black: Natty Bumppo and Chingachgook, Huck Finn and Nigger Jim, Ishmael in bed and on board with Queequeg. The Lone Ranger and Tonto.

It's always been fraternity we've understood, not matrimony. Liberty goes with fraternity. You can't be free sitting in with the wife when there's all the great outdoors. Of course, the wilderness has its dark places where it's scary to be alone. So what's wanted for wandering is a strong and knowing brother. A band of freeborn youths, we'll form, a gang. We broke away from the Mother Country and we won't be tied to apron strings again. It's liberty and fraternity for America.

Our Revolution never did establish the value the French placed centrally, between liberty and fraternity, equality.

So even the brother close by our side must be a lesser brother for all his knowledge or strength, unequal by condition of race. Or of age.

When the young Thoreau went wandering on the water, he was the lesser brother to his big brother John. He spent a week and made a book. And outgrew that kind of union. Yet he never did find a wife. He went to the woods alone.

And that's how it's been in America: if you want the woods, forget the wife. Sell the station wagon and buy a jeep. Come, join the band of brothers.

And then Hassan's car blew up.

Hassan was in the hospital. A student of his was dead.

It's my fault, said Hassan. I had a headache.

Otherwise he would have been driving and the young man, who often got a ride into the City with his teacher, would have been, as usual, in the passenger seat.

I was supposed to be killed, Hassan said, not young Peter. There is no reason for him to be dead.

We knew the SAVAK had done it. Their agents operated openly though illegally in this country. Several times

they had threatened Hassan's life, promising to kill him
if he continued to speak and write about conditions in
Iran.

Hassan had informed the police and the FBI of these
threats. He had written to the Secretary of State. Nothing had been done. It was more nearly in our Government's interest to protect the thugs and assassins of our
despotic ally than the poet and spokesman for human
rights.

We gotta do something, Hope said. This is terrible. Poor
Hassan. Poor, poor Peter.

Maybe if we can find out what kind of device they used,
Jules said. Then we can get to the media.

For some real action, said Anna, we must focus on Peter,
I think, rather than Hassan. Never before has an American citizen been murdered by foreign agents on American
soil. Perhaps that aspect of this outrage will provoke
some action.

I still have the last poems he handed in for my class,
said Ariel. What should I do? To whom should I return
them? Could we publish them, in his memory?

Kill them, he said, massacre the dirty bastards. Cut their
hands off, scalp them. Drag them in the dust behind our
ponies.

We paused at that.

I'm sorry, he said.

Then he began to cry.

č

Peter was buried on a rainy morning.

Hassan was allowed out of the hospital for the funeral. We picked him up. He stood awkwardly on crutches and wore a wide-brimmed hat over his bandages.

The Chief came and Maria deFrise. Fawn Coat had remained behind on guard.

We stood very close together around the open grave. A Rabbi spoke ancient words. After, the boy's mother and father, weeping, came up to us.

Thank you for coming, the father said. You all meant a lot to Peter. He spoke of you very often.

You, the mother said, all of you, you killed him. Teaching him craziness, teaching him not to be satisfied with things. I thought he'd outgrow it. Graduate, get a job, marry. Now, he's dead. And for what? So smart you all are, teachers, you are? You taught him, all right. You taught him good, and now he's dead.

I'm sorry, the father said, leading her away. Please forgive her. She—you understand.

We drove Hassan back to the hospital.

č

I'm sorry about your friend, his wife said. And the boy. I thought maybe you wouldn't come.

He had come again to take his children for the day. He looked at his son, his four-year-old imp, his monkey, his bashful dwarf and ballsy darling. Could he live if they killed his boy?

His daughter said, Daddy, why don't you live with us any more? I don't like Momma's friend. I don't want him for a Daddy.

Don't worry, he said. I'll always be your Daddy. Always, no matter what.

Then stay here, the boy said, you have to stay.

It's like with Ian's Momma and Daddy, his wife said. Like Paula's Mommy and Daddy, remember? This had been explained many times.

And like Jason's and Rachel's, he said.

They could have added more names. In the nursery school and first grade there were not so very many children who had two parents living in the same place.

How would you like to meet some Indians, he said.

Yay, yay, the boy said.

Yuk, said the girl. Who wants to meet some old Indians. That's boring.

Well, he said, one of them is a lady whose name is Fawn Coat. Remember when you liked Bambi? And another lady is named Maria. She's very pretty and has beautiful long hair like yours. Even longer. She wears it in two braids, the way you do sometimes. You'll like her.

Ah, I see, said the wife.

All right, said the girl.

Yay, yay, goody, said the boy.

Just get them home in time for supper, Indians or no, O.K.? I don't want hassles right before bed time. Don't be late, remember, said the wife. Don't make me play the bad guy.

Well, perfesser, said Joey Coniglio, we're waitin on ya, waddaya got to say?

I'm sorry, Joey, but I can't sell.

Hey, c'mon, said Tony Coniglio, you're really gonna get us mad, ya know? I tell ya, take the money an take a walk, or else, ya could end up with nothin an maybe ya won't even be able to walk for a while.

Awright, awright, shh, Tony, be quiet, be nice, said Joey. So what is it now, perfesser, huh? I'm tryin to see your side, ya know? I'm just a plain, ordinary guy, I don't know from nothin too fancy. So tell me plain, O.K., what's the problem? Fifteen grand ain't enough for ya? Awright, O.K., I'm a sport, I'll go to eighteen for ya. There, I said it, everybody heard me, eighteen grand, I'll give ya eighteen grand, an that's my absolute an final offer.

Joey, he said, look, believe me. It's not a question of money.

So what then, said Tony, them mangy Indians? Is that it? You give a shit about them fakes? Don't ya know they're a bunch a hippie dope fiends layin a con on ya? Wait a minute, hey, I got it, ya wanna ball one a them Indian chicks, right? That's it, ain't it! Well, I tell ya, forget it, man, I can tell ya about gook chicks, man, all ya get is a sick dick an a dose a clap. Be smart, tell em to take a bath an go back to the fuckin reservation.

Joey, Tony, listen, he said, I don't want to argue and I don't want you to get mad. I think you're wrong about the Indians up there, but that isn't even the point. For now, I'm not selling to you and I'm not selling to them either. I bought the goddamn piece of land. It's mine and why can't I do what I want with it? So for now, I'm not selling to anybody, and I don't want to talk about it any more.

O.K., perfesser, said Joey, O.K., you got it, no more talk. I don't like wastin my breath neither. On'y, one last thing I gotta tell ya, awright? Do yourself a favor, jus watch your step.

č

Jules got picked up by the FBI.

I told them I didn't have to go with them, he said. I told them to go fuck off.

He had been on his way to the subway when a car pulled up alongside him. Just like in the movies.

FBI, said a clean face out the window. We'd like to talk to you.

I don't have to go with you, said Jules. Talk to yourself.

But two of them got out of the car and blocked his way, and the one who had spoken showed him a gun.

Get in, the gunman said.

Fuck you, Jules said.

Stop or I'll shoot, the gunman said.

Shoot, shoot, you little asshole twerp, Jules said. And he started to walk away.

But they pulled the car up alongside him as he walked and no one shot but someone pushed and another pulled Jules into the car.

They drove to an office building and crowded him up to a room with a desk and some chairs.

This is kidnapping, Jules said, I'll report this to the press. You're holding me against my will. I refuse to talk to you.

Tough tittie, you commie bastard, said one of our Government's agents. Report your little red dick off. We'll deny whatever you say. No one will believe you.

All right then, said another, Who told you to plant that bomb? We know it's you. Which group wanted Hassan Khayil out of the way? Help us and we'll help you. Was it the SL? The PLO? How about the SWP? or RWU? Maybe it was the FLN? BPP? OL? RCP?

This all came about because our Government had been pressured into an investigation of Peter's murder. It did not matter that Hassan had many times reported threats against his life by agents of the SAVAK or that the last threat had come only days before the bombing. An anonymous phone caller had even gone so far as to inform him that Colonel ———, who had overseen his torture in Teheran, was arriving in this country to attend personally to Hassan's demise. Despite all this, it suited our Government better to assume the bombing was the result of squabbling among leftists and radicals.

And so Jules had been picked up.

The SWP! Jules said, Can you imagine! RWU, BPP!

I tell you, when those bastards finally let me go, I couldn't even find an IRT.

*

It was a fine morning just after Christmas. He was on his weekend way to his children when a car pulled up alongside him.

FBI, a man said, Get in.

Hey, you're kidding. C'mon, he said, I don't have to talk to you. You have no right—

Shaddap and get in, another said, opening the back door and pulling him inside.

You can't do this, he said, I know my rights, you—

I thought I tol you shaddap, the man said, and slapped him backhand across the face. Then he pulled a gun and tapped it hard against his cheek.

Now watch, the gunman said to a foreign-looking fellow in dark glasses seated next to the driver. I'll show ya how to handle this kinda thing. Ya don need bombs or nothin fancy. Like this, the cops write him off killed by a mugger. That's how ya want it should look so ain't no way to go make a federal case outa it.

He lunged for the door. They pulled him back and slapped him again.

Hey, said the gunman, poking him in the ribs with the weapon, Jus relax like a good boy, awright? Ain't no one gonna kill you, not today anyways. So jus take it nice an easy.

The car stopped. He saw the East River. He thought they were somewhere under the Williamsburg Bridge.

Out, said the man with the gun.

They walked him into a park. He saw handball courts. There were no players. There were few Sunday strollers, none near by. The gunman behind, flanked by the dark foreigner and the driver, he was crowded into a corner of one of the giant pylons of the Bridge.

O.K., Vito, looks good, the driver said.

So ya see, Colonel, said the gunman, all it takes is a little local knowhow. Pow, he said, pointing the gun.

But he didn't shoot.

Instead the driver hit him, two blows in the lower back and then one across the back of the neck.

He went down, and out.

What did the muggers look like, the cop said.

It wasn't a mugging, he said.

I find you beat up in the park, your wallet's empty, why ain't it a mugging?

He explained how it was.

Sure, O.K., said the cop, have it how you want.

But then he didn't know what kind of car it was and he couldn't describe well what they looked like.

One was called Vito, he said. And Vito called this little dark fellow Colonel.

A colored guy, said the cop.

No, he said, more like some sort of Arab.

Oh, sure, an Ay-rab. Well, whatever you say. But it's the first time I heard the mob had a Ay-rab recruiting office.

He explained again about Joey and Tony and their threats.

O.K., said the cop, O.K. I'll note it down. But, from what you say, even if you ain't crazy, it's probably outa our jurisdiction.

Hassan laughed until it hurt.

But of course there is nothing at all funny about this, Hassan said.

He laughed again.

You have been a belated guinea pig, my friend. Your Ay-rab is my Ay-rab almost surely. The Colonel must have been late in arriving in this country. That is why they used the bomb. Because, as you know, I was also informed in that last phone call that Mafia elements would be involved. I was explicitly told that not SAVAK agents but local experts in the "hit" or "rubout" would be employed so that I could make no political capital out of it. My death was to appear as one more random example of your urban chaos.

I want us to start building my house, he said. We have to do something. Maybe at the very least, in addition to anything else, we can do that. There's got to be some way to have an eye for an eye and also turn the other cheek.

č

His wife, when he'd phoned from the police station, had been pissed. What kind of nonsense was this anyway? He was supposed to come get the kids. She had plans for the afternoon. Now he'd gone and fucked up again. Could she depend on him the following weekend, and any after that?

But then she said, All right, I'm sorry I yelled. Sure, I believe you, even though it's a crazy story. O.K., so it wasn't your fault. You want to tell me more?

Not really, he said. It's not too interesting. I want to start building a house on that land up there.

Can I help? Can I? his son said.

If he can, I want to, too, said his daughter.

Well, O.K., he said, But maybe not right now. We have to figure out a couple of things. Then, once we get it all going, sure you can help, both of you.

Who's the we that's going to be doing the figuring, said his wife.

He named his friends.

I see, she said. A real collection of experts.

Come on, kids, he said, I think it's time for us to get going.

The station wagon and the VW bus headed up the Palisades, changed a flat tire on 9W in Highland Falls, finally went along the Wallkill until the turnoff for his woods.

We had two axes, a hatchet, a bow saw, and grimly good intentions. We planned to pay our respects to the Poquosset, fell a couple of trees, and begin collecting stones for a foundation. Hope had a book published in Vermont that said how to do it. It said anyone could do it. A house growing modestly in the woods might help redress the balance. And, with luck, he could move in on the Fourth of July, like Thoreau before him.

We stopped, but it seemed all wrong. There was no tent. There weren't many trees.

I know this is right, he said. Hey, Jules, isn't this it? Isn't this where we're supposed to be?

Sure it is, said Jules, I'm positive. Only, who took the trees?

And the tent, said Hope, where's the Chief's tipi?

Ariel said, The sweet smell is gone.

They came up in two black Cadillacs, said Maria deFrise. There were maybe four guys in each car. All of them had guns. I ran. We'd left our guns in John's pickup. I guess he went for them. I don't know what Fawn Coat was trying to do.

But the bastards caught them. Two of them held her and slapped her around while the rest of them worked John over. I couldn't do anything. Then they brought up this big flatbed truck with a bulldozer on it. They used chainsaws on the trees and then the 'dozer cleared out the stumps. The 'dozer went over a couple of times and buried everything, wood, brush, stumps, covered the whole thing up and leveled it all out. It was incredible.

When they left, I came out from where I was hiding, got John and Fawn Coat into the pickup, and drove to the hospital in Newburgh. Then I went to the cops. Man, they been paid off or something, the shit they put me through. Hours of questions and the pigs making like they can't believe a word. Then, just to make me feel good, they give me a citation for driving a truck with a busted headlight.

Now we had another hospital to visit.

❦

How are you, *kemo sabe,* said John Whitlock.

I'm O.K., he said. They checked me over at the hospital and let me go. Nothing seems to be broken, I'm just real sore and kind of funny feeling. But, look, Christ, John, how are you? What happened?

We heard the story one more time.

Then John said, My parents, and he motioned to some people standing quietly against the wall. We hadn't even noticed them in our excitement and concern.

And Nelson and Tim Running, John said, my mother's nephews.

The Runnings had identical faces. One wore a business suit and carried an attache case. The other wore long hair in braids and a fringed jacket.

The people you see, John Whitlock said, along with at most a dozen others are the only remaining Poquosset we know of for certain. For now, that's the extent of our tribe. I want you to understand. We aren't even recognized as a tribe by the Bureau of Indian Affairs because we never concluded a single treaty of our own as a separate tribe. The land we consider ours was never much more than several dozen square acres. We fished in the River, we hunted small game in the woods, and we grew corn, beans, and squash.

My father's memory includes the memory of his father and grandfather, but does not include any famous battles we won or lost either with other tribes or with the whites. There were skirmishes of one sort or another and they were bloody enough, but prowess in war never seems to have been that big a deal for the Poquosset. We know of many men and women who were great healers, great hunters, even great warriors. But there is no one you might call a hero, no equivalent of Custer, Miles, or Sheridan, not even one like Geronimo or Sitting Bull or Crazy Horse.

Our history is of the greatest importance to us but it doesn't have the sort of high spots your culture stops to admire. I apologize for the lengthy speech, but I don't want you to delude yourself about us Poquosset. We're not the best kind of Indians to romanticize, if you're going in that direction. I'd like you to see the truth as clearly as you can. Fawn Coat, Maria, me and these people here, a few others, that's it, we're the ones for whom you were beat up.

No, he said, I wasn't beat up for you. I see what you're

telling me, and I'll try to understand. But I want you to see, too. They didn't beat me up because of you. I told them I was keeping the land. Or, that I'd decide in my own good time. I never said anything to make them believe I'd given the land to you. I think that's what I ought to do, though. I think the best thing all around would be to just make the deed over to you.

Well, said John Whitlock, no rush, we'll see, don't worry. Man, you whites are so impulsive! it's no wonder us Indians can't help seeing you as just children, babes in the woods.

č

Henry David Thoreau's last word was Indian.

His next to last word was Moose. Who knows what he meant.

The last book he worked on was to be about Indians. Twenty-five hundred pages of notes for it remain. It was never finished.

In *Walden,* Thoreau wrote, "We need to witness our own limits transgressed, and some life pasturing freely where we never wander."

He wrote a lot of things like that. Maybe Moose and Indian have something to do with that.

Thoreau himself tried to be a free pasturer, poking

around places most of his neighbors would as soon avoid, taking seriously what did not pay. As a young man he went to the waters and a little later to the woods. He lived out his life in town, but even so, he never did find a way to come home comfortably from far pasture. He had no wife. He had no children.

Thoreau died in spring, and through the hard winter we tried to think of spring and take each cold day with an eye to a warmer future.

We watched our friend's life unravel and we hoped each end might in time make a new beginning.

We hoped. We tried to help. We went about our various business separately and together and thought often of the lines in the poem Ariel was now working on

> *Everybody wanted to be good.*
> *No one alive remembered them.*

This was the dead of winter. Nothing grew.

The January thaw didn't come until February that year. Then for more than a week it was hard to believe winter would return. But the groundhog saw his shadow and it didn't lie. Pools of dirty melted snow went hard again to ice. Mud we'd cursed and welcomed froze to unlevel ground.

Ariel twisted her ankle and hobbled around with a cane for weeks. Hope missed a couple of classes, having chanced a weekend in Vermont and failed to get out before a snow.

Jules organized a faculty-student symposium on the multi-national corporations. Anna and her son both were speakers. We learned in detail with slides how many of the world's people danced to the corporate tune; we saw from tables and charts the cost in pain to make a profit.

We brought out a limited edition of Peter's poems by

subscription. Anna had selected an epigraph from Brecht; Hassan contributed a preface and a memorial poem. Peter's father sent a note of thanks. Others to whom we'd sent copies—the Secretary of State, the New York *Times*, the Democrat and Republican for President—did not respond.

We had enjoyed the thaw. It was winter that went on.

č

His children when he saw them seemed poorly. His wife looked tired.

It's February, she said, what can you expect from February? No wonder it's the shortest month. A little longer and it would kill us. Where are you taking the kids?

I don't know, he said. I'm sorry, I meant to check the *Post* for children's entertainment, but I just didn't get to it.

He rose to be leaving, expecting disgust and anger at another instance of his incompetence.

She shook her head and waved her hand.

That's O.K., she said. Sit down. You want a drink?

He sat down on the edge of a bench he had made a long time ago.

Sure, he said. What do you have in the house nowadays?

You mean what does *he* drink, she said.

He stood up again.

Come on, come on, she said. What do you want? Bourbon? wine?

Bourbon, he said.

No ice for you, right?

Right. Just straight.

The kids were playing nicely in the other room. He looked to see if they were getting restless, impatient to be going. He had been on the street with them within fifteen minutes of his arrival every time since the split-up. Now he sat. The kids played nicely.

Cheers, his wife said.

Yeah, he said.

What news of the mobsters?

Nothing. I don't know, not a thing. It's a little scary.

And your Indians?

Oh, they're O.K., I guess. Or maybe not so good. The

whole thing's going to be in the courts for quite awhile. By the way, I guess I might as well talk to you now about this. I want to sign the land over to them, to the Indians. I mean, I'm not forgetting that it isn't even really mine, that—

Yeah, well, she said, that's O.K. Go ahead. It's probably best. I never cared much about that land anyway.

I know, he said, but I did. I still do. Look, I'm sorry about how I pressured you, and all. It was important to me. It's still important to me, even now. But, you know, maybe if I hadn't—

No, she said. It wasn't that. Not only that. Hey, you want another drink?

No, he said. No, thanks. I guess I'd better just get the kids and go.

Sure, she said, O.K. They're all ready except to put on their coats. Maybe when you guys get back.

Yeah, he said, O.K. I'd like that.

Preparations for America's big birthday party went on apace. Day by day we felt more sure we weren't invited.

The contest for President also went on. For the Election party we all but Hassan had our invitations—by birthright, or, in Anna's case, by naturalization. But maybe we'd stay home from that one, too.

Ariel might stay home because the suffering of the Poet could not be assuaged by a mere change in Administration.

Jules would surely stay home because as a Marxist he could hardly be expected to participate in the legitimization of bourgeois institutions. He would have nothing to do with the farce of electoral politics. It was nothing to the point that the publisher for his books was a subsidiary of ITT or that his last academic employer had been entirely funded by the State.

Hassan would have to stay home. As a noncitizen he was not allowed to vote, although as a nonwhite native of the Third World he could not have brought himself to vote in any case. Neither of the two candidates would move to curb the corporations in their rape of the earth, their pollution of the atmosphere, their repression of every effort to be whole and free. For the people of his country and for poor peoples everywhere this election was largely meaningless.

The rest of us generally concurred in some version of the poetical and political reasons for avoiding the Election party, though we knew all the same that, in the end, we might go to the polls, unable, finally to stay home. We were certain of how much suffering the Republican fellow could inflict, and we were no more than almost certain of the other fellow's capacity in this direction. So, though Jules might stay home, or Ariel, the rest of us who could, with a longing to believe in the difference even a small difference might make, would probably go and vote.

č

Ah, you fantasy-land radicals, John said. Of course you must vote. Though I grant you, it's the very least thing to do. We have to find ways to use this election to our advantage, get one of those guys to come out for us and for the rights of Native Americans.

To this end, he'd written to each of the two who might win. And before long, he got his replies.

The Incumbent President sent a letter which began

The heritage of the Native American is indeed rich and his traditions are proud. Indian culture has made important contributions to all we know and value in America today. There is no one who can be unaware how indebted were our Fore-fathers. . . .

It got worse for three pages and never mentioned the issue of the Poquosset's fight for their ancestral land.

The Challenging Candidate opened his letter in a man-ner designed to illustrate his campaign's repeated com-mitment to Openness and Honesty. He wrote

I am extremely pleased to have this opportunity to respond to you personally concerning the im-portant questions not only legal but moral in

nature which you raise. Frankness and trust between Government and the governed, in particular
between Red Man and White, has too often been
avoided.

Promising as this might seem, the Challenger's pleasure
in responding was not of the kind to move him to any
definite position on the important questions raised.
Frankly and in all honesty, he admitted they were indeed
complex. If elected, he would, of course, do all in his
power to see that Justice Was Done.

Then John called a press conference.

But no reporters came.

A number of us, Indians, friends, and supporters, went
up to Albany and sat in at the Governor's office. But the
Governor had just left for Washington. His aides would
neither talk to us nor call the police. When the cops came
(we called them), they wouldn't arrest us. Not even the
local media ran the story. So, as far as the world knew,
nothing had happened.

Let us not be despondent, John said. We must continue
to do what we can, both with the Election and also with
the Bicentennial. Our plans for a Centennial Celebration
are coming along. I've heard from some Seneca who want
to be involved, and Nelson's law firm has just sent him
on an assignment out west. He'll have a chance to con-
tact some Sioux and Cheyenne friends personally. They're
sure to want to help us commemorate Custer's defeat.

And we'll tie it in to the Election, too, because if not for the Indians, Custer might have gone on to be President. He had the vanity, he had the will, he even had the backing. If the fight on the Greasy Grass didn't turn things around for the Indians, maybe it still changed history a lot more than people know.

That all sounds fine, said Hope, but, ya know, this Birthday business is getting to be such a big deal, you have to make sure you don't get typed as just a bunch of spoilsports.

Hope is quite right, Anna said. The Americans believe themselves an innocent, funloving people. It is very difficult to make them understand that you are taking action *for* something, that you are not just against a good time.

Already the media has valuable experience at making dissidence out to be neurotic grumpiness, Jules said. They're very adept at presenting even the best-reasoned opposition as no more than a bad case of grouch.

And yet, said Anna, you will remember that it was just the opposite they did during the Viet Nam years. At that time our opposition to the War was discredited by making us out to be a wild pack of fun-loving idiots, demonstrating only as an excuse to get stoned and have sex. The media was very selective in its coverage of domestic dissent. And how could the Country take the clowns it saw on tv seriously? how could people be expected to believe us rather than the President of the United States.

You're right, said Ariel. But it seems incredible that people could really have thought those thousands and thousands of us who gathered time after time were just roving bands of hippies. I'm almost flattered to think it, but how could anyone imagine people like us as savages in beads and feathers?

Just a bunch of wild Indians, he said, race traitors. Crackpots and cranks on the side of the Red and the Yellow, against the White.

It's an old story, man, Maria said. One way or another, America forgets about us until it's time for someone to take the rap. Then there's always the dumb Indian. Take this Revolution of yours they're promoting now. How did they all dress up, that gang of whites who made your famous Boston Tea Party? not as British soldiers or a bunch of old ladies. They got themselves up as Indians to pretend it was the painted dumb savages dumped the tea in Boston Harbor. All that stuff you hear about stamps and taxes, that's mostly crap, man. It was to inflame opinion against the Indians that they got that act together.

There's a lot to that, Fawn Coat said, because, you know, bad as British treatment of Native Peoples in America was, it was considerably better than what we got from the Colonists. It was the British who ordered no further expansion on Indian lands west of the Appalachians. And it was to rip off that land that you Colonials provoked the Revolution.

But, really, said Hassan, this is fascinating! I've never

heard these things! You can't imagine what a different picture of your American Revolution is painted by the history books in Iran.

Yes, Hassan, we said. Oh, yes, we can.

č

Goddam it, said Maria, just what the hell am I doing here with you?

He said nothing.

You went through the blacks and the Vietnamese in the 'sixties, and now it's the 'seventies, and you're bored with them, right? So now it's us Indians, right?

He said nothing.

That's all it is, right, she said.

Then she said, It was nice to meet your kids.

My daughter thought you were beautiful, he said.

I'm glad, she said, but still. I mean, what is it, what the hell is this, that I'm here with you?

Come on, Maria, he said, listen, will you please just cut the shit? O.K.? What're you doing, what am I doing, I'll tell you what we're doing, we're having one of those stupid conversations people sometimes have in bed, that's what we're doing. But, you know, what we were doing just a few minutes ago was clear enough. After all, if you want to go on about it, what the hell am I doing here with you? I ask you now, frankly, as one Vanishing American to another.

Fuck you, she said.

But she laughed.

Fuck you, too, he said.

And they did.

č

He hadn't heard from the Coniglio Brothers.

He tried to believe they had forgotten about him. He knew he hadn't forgotten about them.

One afternoon he found himself on Thompson Street in front of Renzo's Bar. His feet had taken him there from Eighth Street where he'd gone to buy books. He hadn't consulted his head. The books were under his arm.

He went in and sat down at the bar. He ordered a beer. Joey Coniglio was there, in a booth. He hadn't dared plan it this way. It was as if he had.

There was a guy in work clothes sitting opposite Joey. Before Joey noticed him, he thought some things about this guy.

He thought this guy operated a bucketloader or backhoe or steam shovel. He was tanned and wore a hat, and he thought this guy never took his hat off except in church. He kept his tan through the meanest winter. He had all his hair. He would always have his hair. He smoked cigarettes down to the very end but he wouldn't get cancer. This guy wouldn't. The pay was good for what he did but that wasn't why he loved his work. He loved his work because of the sense of mastery it gave; the right light touch upon the levers could move mountains. This guy had the touch. Joey was his boss but he bowed to no one. So he wasn't ever upset. He was calm; he always was calm. What could be worth his worry?

So when Joey noticed him and invited him to come over, having thought these things about this guy, it was O.K. He smiled. He said, Hi, Joey.

Joey sent the guy away, and he got up and took his beer and slid into the booth across from Joey Coniglio.

So look who's here. So how ya been, perfesser?

He shrugged his shoulders.

Awright, awright, sure, I can unnerstan yer sore. Nobody likes to get roughed up. Look, ya think I like to have to do that to a guy? But, you, you are one goddam stubborn sonofabitch. What the hell ya expect me to do?

He shrugged his shoulders.

Geez, perfesser, yer a real talker today, aincha. Well, so,

look, if ya ain got nothin to say, what're ya doin here?
Ya get a sudden irresistible thirst or somethin?

I don't know what I'm doing here, Joey. I didn't even
know I was going to come over here. Yeah, sure, I guess
I wanted to see you, all right. But I don't know what to
say.

Listen, I'll tell ya what to say. Say ya decided to sell me
that lousy piece a property a yours that's causin so
much trouble. That's what ya should say.

Yeah, I know. But, look, I'm sorry, Joey, I can't. I'm
going to make the title over to John Whitlock and the
Poquosset Tribe.

Yer kiddin me. Ya got to be kiddin, aincha? Why would
ya wanna go an do a stupid thing like that for? Them
blanketheads ain't got no money, so it can't be the money.
Anyhow, you're such a classy guy, a guy like you, a little
thing like money don't mean nothin to ya anyway. Ya
think yer doin a good deed or some shit like that? Lemme
tell ya, Mister Perfesser, them Indians ain gonna get
that land no matter what, so how ya like that? One way
or another, legal in the courts, or a little pressure here
an there, I'm tellin ya I'm gonna get it, me, Joey
Coniglio, Coniglio Brothers, Inc., Construction. That's
right, me an Tony, an my people, we got some big plans,
an we ain about to let no egghead or no freaky Indians
come along an fuck us over, ya hear? Awright, so
awright, now ya tol me. So is that it, or ya got some other
good news ya wanna gimme?

He shook his head and shrugged his shoulders. And continued to sit.

Geez, I swear couldn' nobody blame me if I set the gorillas on ya again jus to teach ya a lesson. Man, Tony's liable to do that anyways, when he hears about this. Cause ya know, ya know what ya gone an done, ya gone an messed up my little brother's birthday present. Yeah, that's right. You heard I told him I was gonna start diggin right on his birthday. You think we ain got feelins too? Ha? Ah, what the hell, so the lawyers'll handle it. Believe it, perfesser, there're ways.

Look, Joey, will you tell me, why do you want it so bad? What is it about just that little piece of land?

It ain just that piece, perfesser. You wouldn't unnerstan. That's just a part of it, it's a whole big deal, up there, with zoning an sewage lines, an a atomic power plant we maybe heard somethin about. Like this, like that, one thing an another. We need it, that's all. Lemme tell ya, I got people I got to answer to, ya know? Ya put my ass in a sling, too, with all this cockamamie stuff a yours. So willya look at how he's grinnin, all of a sudden there? Hey, what the fuck you smilin at like that, huh? What'd ya drop yer marbles or somethin? Geez, I swear, perfesser, I wish I'd a never met you. Hey, hey, Angie, c'mere, bring this nutcase an me two more.

The drinks came. They drank.

So listen, nutcase, waddaya say, you maybe hungry? It's

gettin late, how about we go get some clams? You eat clams or there's somethin wrong with that too? Awright, good, so c'mon, I'll take ya someplace. Geez, willya put yer money away? Angie'll put it on my tab. I swear, I don't know what the hell I'm doin, ya musta made me crazy or somethin. Here I should kill the dumb bastard an I'm gonna feed him clams. Cause, listen, perfesser, no offense, but you are, ya really are dumb, what you're givin away. Now don go gettin sore again, awright? Let's jus go have some clams. On'y, hey, look, do me a favor, willya? Quit smilin at me like that? Especially in this fuckin neighborhood, I swear, people'll think we're a couple a fruits or somethin.

❦

But his wife called a few days later and said the children were missing.

She cried and her voice broke. When she'd called the school, they told her the kids' uncle had picked them up. The uncle they described sounded a lot like Tony Coniglio.

He drove into the City. With his wife at their apartment was a flat-faced fellow she introduced as Bill. He didn't think she'd ever called the lover by name before. Bill had already telephoned the police.

We're waiting, Bill said. We haven't heard anything.

Make yourself a drink, his wife said. Take whatever you want. She started to cry.

Both men leaned toward her with arms outstretched to comfort. Both refrained from touch. There was no etiquette for such occasions. He wanted to be good. And felt a fool.

They waited. They drank.

He called Renzo's Bar and asked for Joey. Angie the barman said Joey who. He never heard of no Joey Coniglio.

He realized he knew of no home or business address, no phone number for the Coniglios. He wanted to do something; with the wife and the lover, he drank and sat, drank and stood and paced about the room.

The police came for photos of the kids. His wife described what they'd been wearing today. He offered descriptions of Joey and Tony.

It grew dark.

Several times, not wanting to make a nuisance of himself but unable to do no more than wait, he called the police. There was no news. They advised he not tie up the lines and assured him they would call as soon as anything was known.

He thought of Peter who had been blown up. He thought of Hassan fearing for his children. He hated Bill who was not the father.

I hear you're building a house, Bill said.

Sort of. I was planning to, he said.

Construction, yeah, that's nice work, Bill said. I used to do that kind of work before I came to New York. Just use your muscles and don't think about anything all day. I hired out to contractors by day and wrote at night. It's a good balance, you know? I never needed much sleep anyway. Lucky that way, I guess.

Yeah, he said, I guess.

Bill talked some more. His wife said a word now and again. He realized he knew who Bill was. He'd just published a novel, his second. It was very long and serious. The reviews were very long and serious. It sounded kind of artsy for his taste, but probably real work.

Untrue to his principles, he hoped it would not sell. He swore to himself he would not read it ever, not all the way through, anyway.

So, if you need a hand with any of it, Bill said, just let me know.

What? he said.

I mean like framing it out, or setting windows, or something. I'd be glad to help.

Yeah. Thanks.

His wife said, Anyone want another drink?

He did. Bill did, too.

You have two beautiful kids, Bill said. Really, you're a lucky man. I think kids are great.

Mnn, he said.

No, really, I do. I mean, your daughter and me, for instance, I think we get on terrific together, I really do.

O.K., he said, enough. You want me to kill you now or should I make an appointment for some place else?

As he stood up and took two wobbly steps, as Bill stood up, and the wife stepped between, the phone rang. The police.

The kids were all right. They had just walked into a station house in a Brooklyn precinct. The Brooklyn cops would drive them home. Probably they were on their way home already.

The kids arrived tired and wide awake, cranky and full of talk. The boy was especially interested in cops and guns. He had actually held one of the cops' guns. So he said. The girl alternated between pleasure and upset. This had clearly been an adventure—but of what sort, she, thoughtful, wasn't sure. The best part was they'd had supper at McDonald's.

A man had picked them up at school. He said he was a friend of their mother's. She hadn't mentioned anything, but they had had a number of different baby-sitters, men and women, since their parents' split, and were trying to learn not to be surprised by a new face. The man was nice. He drove them around for awhile; then they went for sodas and ice cream. They stopped at a house somewhere to go to the bathroom and watch cartoons on television. Then they went to McDonald's. They drove around some more and then the man pulled up in front of a police station. He'd told them to go in the door. He'd said their mother would be inside to pick them up.

She hadn't been. But the cops paid a lot of attention and soon they were home. They didn't understand. But, in all, it wasn't so bad.

With a washcloth, then pajamas, he helped get them ready for bed. They said good night. Then they called for him to come and tuck them in.

Bill sat in the living room drinking, smiling, not leaving.

Will you be here in the morning, his son said.

Will you make us breakfast like you used to, his daughter said.

Stay, stay, they said.

In several places he felt his heart break.

Kids, he said, I can't. But I promise, I'll pick you up from school tomorrow. I'll take off from work, O.K.? He kissed them and turned out the light.

He rejoined Bill and his wife. He knew he couldn't stay.
He didn't want to leave first.

Look, his wife said, thanks. But, could you both just
go now? I've got to get some sleep. O.K.? Please?

Thanks, she said.

Goodnight, he said.

Goodnight, Bill said.

Goodnight, he said.

č

It took him four hours to get to Newburgh. It wasn't
traffic. What slowed him down was trying to go fast. He
had an accident. Hit a zebra-striped van in the ass. The
kid driving was stoned, sympathetic. No big deal, man,
he said. He passed over a joint. Anyway, he said, like,
I ain't got no insurance on this thing, you dig?

They pulled, each his vehicle, to the side of the road. He
sat with the kid in the van, smoking pot and listening
to music loud.

You and the night and the music, he said. He giggled.

Right, man, heavy. What's it from?

He nodded his head. Right, he said.

Then it occurred to him the station wagon was drivable. He had, to the side of the road behind the van, driven it.

Well, I'll see ya, he said.

Take care, man, the kid said, there's weirdos everywhere.

He knew where Maria lived but not the exact address, and made a nuisance of himself in several houses before finding her at last.

After a few false starts he made himself clear, although he could not quite see clarity as a virtue.

My kids, he said, my wife. My kids, oh, god, my kids.

Maria undressed him and got him into bed.

Try to sleep, she said.

But he wanted to make love.

He hadn't got his house built. Hadn't even turned the other cheek let alone got an eye for an eye. So he wanted now to make love.

Potency was the problem, how to get it up in the world.

Go to sleep, Maria said. Shh, try to sleep now. It's all right, go to sleep.

It wasn't all right.

He lay there wide awake.

Near dawn he couldn't even do that any more. And fell asleep at last.

č

When he said he wanted to die, we said nothing.

He looked at each of us in turn.

The radio was on in the other room, the news. He got up and went and turned it off.

I will not hear of the gunmen of the world, he said. The pests are here, the rats are out. The chickens have come home to roost. There was a time to build up, but now is a time to tear down. Hand me a bow, build me a bomb, I want to kill, he said. I want to die.

Please, said Ariel, please, don't. It's over now, almost over. Even the winter's nearly done. All of it, it's got to pass. Please, please don't.

They took my kids, he said. Get me a gun, give me an axe, sharpen my scalping knife. I'm going for blood, I want to kill.

He paused.

My mind is gone, he said. I want to die.

You must try to remember your children are all right,

said Anna. You must not indulge yourself. What happened was a most unfortunate thing. But your children did not really suffer. They are all right and they will not be bothered again.

That's right, said Jules, remember? Come on, I told you, I found those guys, I talked to them. They wouldn't admit anything, of course, but they were both very repentant. It was the kid brother, the hothead, he's the one snatched the kids. Joey hadn't told him about seeing you, that you were going to sign the title over to the Indians. They're working on a job up in Yonkers, I was able to trace them. I told you.

Yeah, but—

Of course, Tony's got ten people who'll swear he was anywhere he says he was, so there's no question of bringing charges. The cops wouldn't hold them on just the kids' say-so. But that's not the point. The thing is, this has gotten way out of hand and they aren't happy about it. They don't want any trouble, no police nosing around, no newspaper guy getting interested. Legitimacy's the name of the game these days, and these guys don't want to attract any more attention than they have to.

Yeah, but—

And, look, Joey, the older one, he seemed to feel especially bad about it. He says he's got three kids of his own and something about the two of you drinking and going for clams. I didn't know what the hell he was talking about, except that this kind of thing won't happen again. They're still plenty pissed at you about the piece of property. Joey even sort of halfheartedly asked if maybe you wouldn't change your mind and sell after all. But, anyway, they're just going to let their lawyers handle it, so that should be that. You're O.K., your kids are O.K.

It is a thing worth to know, said Hassan. Listen to what Jules tells you and take heart. I cannot know my children will be safe. I cannot see them even so much as once a week. It is too dangerous. But I am pleased to know at least that your children are no longer in danger. You must try to be pleased to know it too.

Also, said Hope, your wife called. She wanted me to make sure and tell you the kids were fine, no problems. But she was worried about you. She said, if you wanted, to give her a call and come and have supper with her and the kids.

And you had at least three calls from Maria, Anna said. She's been trying to reach you all day. She said to tell you John is going to drive her in to the City and she'd try to call you when she gets here. This is the number where they'll be, if you want to call. All the Poquosset are very upset about what happened and that you are suffering on their behalf.

When I asked her, said Ariel, Maria told me that the ice is melted in the River. The ground is beginning to thaw. John will bring us a freshly dug basket of Jerusalem artichokes. I can cook them up and if you'd like we can have supper together tonight, all of us.

What are these things from Jerusalem, said Hassan. I don't think I have ever heard of them.

That's because they're not from Jerusalem, Hope said. Got nothing to do with Jerusalem, so far's I know. The name's a corruption of *girasole*, Italian for sunflower. It's a perennial sunflower, you eat the tubers. *Girasole* fell off somebody's tongue and landed as Jerusalem. But they're very American.

They're wonderful, said Ariel. You can boil them, or slice them and fry them, or cut them raw into salads. They taste a little like water chestnuts.

Right, Hope said, they're great. I got em growing all over the place in Vermont. They spread like crazy. You can pickle em, bake em, even make a nice white wine out of em.

I hear they give you gas, though, said Jules.

Stop, he said, for Christ's sake, stop it, will you? Tell John to bring me a tomahawk, not a basket of roots. What are you all carrying on like maniacs for? That creep is still in my house, with my wife, with my kids. Can you understand what I'm saying? He's there with my kids and I'm here. And I'll tell you something else, his book, his novel, that shits too. I don't know, my mind's gone. I have to kill somebody, even if it's only me. And you all sit here chattering about baking and boiling and frying. I have to kill. I want to die.

But we knew he didn't want to die. He wanted to live. Only he didn't know how.

č

American men have got to learn carelessness and special-ization from the moment of their birth if they want to get on in the world. To push the other guy aside, to take the *Times* each morning at breakfast with no loss of appetite, and hurry off; to leave the house and the kids, the art and politics and ethics, to women, hobbyists, and misfits so all the narrowed self can concentrate on climb-ing the ladder of success as near to the top as force and luck (and birth and prior condition of servitude) allow. This was the lesson of our history so far, what more than two hundred years had come to, doin right or doin wrong. It was the Puritans who had won, not the Indians; the Businessmen, not the Poets.

But he'd cared too much and about too many things, dis-persing what energies he had. He couldn't seem to choose between the forest and the trees—on principle, he some-times thought; out of weakness, pure personal deficiency he now deeply felt. Still, he knew his loyalty was to the losers. No wonder he said he wanted to die.

Because he didn't know better than the Indians how to live as an Indian. He didn't know better than Thoreau how to live as a Poet.

To live as an Indian meant to live in a measure of harmony with the world. There is no story of a Fall in

Indian myth or legend. No god of the Indians gave man only an act of disobedience as his sole opportunity for innovation in the newmade world. Every tribe had stories about First Man's foolishness or error or arrogance. But there is nothing like Sin.

So the ground was never cursed for the Indians; Nature is not corrupt. No god of theirs ever drove them from the place he had just troubled to make for them. There is no restlessness or rootlessness, no nostalgia for a loss that cannot be made good this side of Heaven. It was wholly consistent with honor to say a simple Yes to the world.

Whereas our friend, year in, year out, said No. It wasn't at all that he took pleasure in opposition. For how, in our world, could a man say Yes with honor? With honor—with principle; consistent with a sense of decency, integrity, character: all the old words for value, the qualities that the times had discarded?

And yet he longed for reconciliation. He was a great many years past adolescence when opposition was a bitter joy and anxious release. Now he wanted to say Yes and await his reward. For opposition which gives an appetite also takes its toll. How fine it would be, how restful, to say, Sure, count me in; to go along with everyone else. To stand *with* and not against.

But for our friend, as for ourselves, always the price of peace was too high. He could not say Yes if it meant complete surrender, the gain in ease purchased only at the loss of—honor: integrity, character, decency. The place made for us had been taken away and we would have to make a place for ourselves before we could say Yes again. Before we could live in relation to our world as the Indians had lived to theirs.

The only trouble was the Indians hadn't managed to live that way and still to live.

To live that way was also what Thoreau had meant by living as a Poet: to live in accord, with honor. To act in a way consistent with one's best thought; to unify theory and practice. To live wholly, without narrow specializing, without vast carelessness.

But Thoreau's world was very nearly our world. So for all his desire also to say Yes, like us, like our friend, his sense of honor demanded that he mostly say No.

A persistent No was the matter of work. Even a Poet has to get his living. A man should work at what he does best, Thoreau assumed; and he thought walking the woods and huckleberrying were probably his surest talents. But of course no one would pay him for that. He went to Harvard, graduated, class of '37, with a number of careers open to him, the usual paths taken by Cambridge men of his time. He could have been a minister, a lawyer, a merchant, a doctor, or a teacher.

Thoreau was hardly one to give himself in service to the God of the Church or the Laws of the State, so neither the pulpit nor the bar could give him a living consistent with his principles. "In my experience nothing is so opposed to poetry . . . as business," he was to write in his Journal. And though there were times he would work for money alone, the regular service of Mammon was not for him. He could not be a merchant. There was no principle standing in the way of medicine. But there his temperament was averse. Thoreau became a teacher.

The schoolroom was no refuge from the world. Within a month the School Committee made clear to him that he must flog unruly students. Thoreau was against it and it was a principle he wouldn't compromise. Life without principle is no life, not for a Poet and not for a man. Perhaps to show he was no sentimentalist, he whipped his class one time. Then he quit. You can't think one way and act another. Even if it costs you your living. Better lose the living and save the life. Even if it throws you out of work.

Or in to prison.

Or off to the woods.

For in this regard Thoreau was no Puritan, no Christian, either, for that matter: Nature was for him as if uncursed. There was no taint or stain of Sin on any truths she might reveal. Maybe in the woods if not among men he could live in harmony and not in opposition. Somewhere there had to be where a man could say Yes and not be ashamed. Even from the woods Thoreau took walks into town, his ties with the world not wholly severed. In the woods he consolidated his vision, found himself. Then he moved back to Concord village. His middle life he lived among men. Those years filled up again and again with No.

But it probably wasn't for love of opposition in Thoreau either. The cause he worked for and went to jail for was the abolition of slavery. But it was the Indian who held his imagination, to whom he'd looked early and to whom he returned late. Thoreau's last journey, his last planned work, his last spoken word were all the same.

It was to Thoreau and to Indians that our friend again and again returned, our friend who said he wanted to die. Our friend who had wanted woods and wife and now had neither.

We'd told him there was no American precedent for the wholeness he wanted. Hassan, we'd said, of any one we knew, had come the closest. But Hassan was not an American; in certain ways his example did not quite locally count.

We'd meant no more than to state the lesson writ large by our history, to point out the plain fact by which we'd lasted for two hundred years. In all that time, Thoreau was probably the best in the wholeness line America had managed. And even he hadn't known how to have both woods and wife, although he'd surely wanted both.

Thoreau started out like the American boy, with liberty and fraternity and his week on the water. But when he came ashore, matrimony was on his mind. He asked young Ellen Sewall to be his wife, but she refused. He seems next to have fallen in love with Lidian Emerson, but she was his friend's wife. So when he felt it was time to go to the woods, he went alone.

He began his experiment at Walden on the Fourth of July and carried it forward for two years before moving back to the world. He had a great talent for wanting little, but couldn't quite make a whole life out of solitude. He knew who he was, after the woods; now he wanted a world to inhabit.

He wanted it and he found it. But he couldn't much say Yes to it. His country, our country, permitted slavery as the law of the land; it invaded Mexico as it would invade Viet Nam and Cambodia. To this Thoreau could not decently say Yes. Again and again he said No. But his refusal to pay his tax, his night in jail, his angry speeches to his neighbors did not stop the War nor set the slaves free.

And at the end of it all, his final word was Indian. So maybe even as Thoreau died in opposition, maybe his continued hope was still, as always, for reconciliation, for harmony. And so he named the only ones he knew whose relation to the world had seemed one of assent.

Maybe his last private word was a Yes as his last public act had been a further No. For Thoreau had spoken out in praise of John Brown at a time when even most Northerners reviled him.

Henry Thoreau couldn't help but see the old man's raid

on Harper's Ferry as anything but the full enactment of principle, practice in strictest accord with honorable belief. That raid didn't set the slaves free either. But the man who carried it out (his name was also John, like Thoreau's father's and his older brother's; and he, too, died leaving Henry alive in confusion and pain), this John Brown re-awakened all the strength of that Thoreau who had always been fierce in his desire to live as a Poet.

Because, for most of the years after he left Walden, Henry David Thoreau had not quite managed to live as a Poet. Perhaps, for him, too, prolonged opposition had taken its toll. Thoreau, in his middle years, had lived less as a Poet than as Nature's fussy tailor, taking her measurements with great and greater care, and yet somehow unable to sew the cloth. He earned his living mostly by surveying, walking the boundaries of woodlots and pasturelands. Then he would make notes in his Journal, compiling lists and planning projects, but never able to integrate, to complete anything that could touch his earlier work.

But then for John Brown he could find the words. And what he said of Brown, that he did not die, is true of Thoreau himself.

"On the day of his translation," Thoreau wrote

> I heard, to be sure, that he was *hung*, but I did not know what that meant; I felt no sorrow on that account; but not for a day or two did I even *hear* that he was *dead*, and not after any number of

days shall I believe it. Of all the men who were said to be my contemporaries, it seemed to me that John Brown was the only one who *had not died*. I never hear of a man named Brown now,—and I hear of them pretty often,—I never hear of any particularly brave and earnest man, but my first thought is of John Brown, and what relation he may be to him. I meet him at every turn. He is more alive than he ever was. He has earned immortality. He is not confined to North Elba nor to Kansas. He is no longer working in secret. He works in public, and in the clearest light that shines on this land.

It was on another Fourth of July, in 1860, that those words were read.

And what Thoreau said about John Brown, said about himself, Seathl, Chief of the Dwamish, said of the Indians:

When the last Red Man shall have perished, and the memory of my tribe shall have become a myth among the White Men, these shores will swarm with the invisible dead of my tribe, and when your children's children think themselves alone in the field, the store, the shop, upon the highway, or in the silence of the pathless woods, they will not be alone. At night when the streets of your cities and villages are silent and you think them deserted, they will throng with the returning hosts that once filled and still love this beautiful land. The White Man will never be alone.

> Let him be just and deal kindly with my people,
> for the dead are not powerless. Dead, did I say?
> There is no death, only a change of worlds.

Unlike Thoreau, we had failed to take Indians into account when we spoke of the lesson of our history. Maybe it was ignorance, or that ingrained racism that even the most careful Americans don't easily escape. Who were we to say that Indians were not available as an American model? All the great chiefs were married men who had performed their life adventures not as astronauts (the exploit *out there* in space, the wife and kids on earth), and not as adolescents (on the raft with a pal, the whole domestic culture, with the women, bound to land), but as grown men, not even young, their wives and children close by them. Certainly they had never separated wife and woods.

So Indians, if they could not be blueprints, might be models.

Only they had not, as Indians, survived.

Our friend wished John Whitlock and his Poquosset well, but anything they would achieve was bound to be no longer just Indian but some new synthesis of white and red. Theirs might be a future informed by the past; it could not be again what once it was. Never again could Indians be a people living within the hoop, in an unbroken circle, in harmony with their world. For if Indian legend had no story of a Fall, Indian history had: it occurred when the whitemen came. Columbus and Cortes and Coronado, Ralegh and Lord Baltimore, Winthrop and Bradford. They were the snakes in the Garden.

He knew all this. Still he wished for wholeness, for what he had been calling wife and woods. Like the Indians. Like Thoreau.

But now our friend who once had said his name was Henry, could only say, I want to die.

He meant he wanted to live but did not know how.

I want to die, he said.

But he didn't want to die. Only to change worlds.

He wouldn't say he wanted to go to the woods.

We waited. Those who could made jokes. We kept our ears open. He said nothing. What we heard made no one laugh.

In Uganda a uniformed madman sat on top. He said that Hitler was his hero. Not to be outdone by any whiteman, he'd set to giving genocide new meaning. Available for his purpose were more than the twelve tribes of Israel.

Thus Uganda. Also, South Africa and Rhodesia. Lebanon and Eritrea. Northern Ireland and South Korea. It was a merry world. The guns went bang and the jails were full. The torturers worked overtime and still the flood rolled on of those in need of torture. Around the world they came in whole and went out broken to serve as an example, to serve as a reminder that in some places it was not only wearying to live in opposition.

We let the news voice go on. He listened unmoved or did not hear. We watched. We waited. No one joked.

He wouldn't say a thing.

č

Do you think you might be able to do me a favor, said Hassan.

I guess so, he said, sure. What is it?

You don't teach on Friday, is that right?

Right.

And, if it should become necessary, do you think you could miss class on Monday?

I suppose so. I'd have to make it up. But, look, what's this all about?

And your car, how is it? It runs well, just now? Everything is all right?

It's O.K. I just keep it filled and change the oil a lot, that seems to do it. But—

Good, very good. Now just one thing more, I must ask you. If this favor I speak of, if it should involve, let us say, a bit of risk, would you still consider it?

Come on, Hassan, he said, what the hell is all this? My car, my schedule, risk, what are we talking about?

Good, said Hassan, very good. I see I have your attention.

č

His kids looked better, spring and all. Now the weather was warmer they played outside. It showed in their cheeks. With kids you could see the correlation.

His wife looked terrible.

She was the one who mostly took them out. But with her there was no correlation visible.

I think you lost some weight, he said.

I don't know, she said, maybe.

That used to be a compliment; perhaps not now. What had gone had departed the face, not waist or hips. And there were dark patches under her eyes.

And you, she said, I can't tell any more. How are you?

He said as best he could.

And Pocahontas? How's your Indian Princess?

He stood, turned away to get the kids.

Behind him he heard her cry.

Look, she said, I'm sorry, whatever you think, you can bet I promise myself not to say that kind of thing. Only then—

She was crying again. He came back and sat down.

That's O.K., he said, I know how it is. You know, there are lots of things I try not to say to you.

Well, maybe you should, she said, maybe you should say them.

Maybe, he said, maybe I should.

Now that we didn't go to the woods we thought we might try to grow something right where we were. Vegetables we had in mind which took only a little dirt indoors or out. Even in the City spring signs were sure, new green and buds irrefutable. We thought to put in some seed.

Growing your own food, even a tiny part of it, gives a sense of the connection between origins and ends, testifies to causality with edible effects. It was a tribute to future-confidence to trust the dry hard hopeless-looking seed to the ground, and think something might come up. Yet in time something usually does come up. And there you are, a tomato in a pot on a fire escape, a couple of zucchini plants or a few stalks of corn in a vacant lot: in the City these are real flags of Independence and not just on the Fourth of July.

But City-grown vegetables are probably not good for us because of all the poisons they've taken in to make their growth. From the debris-laden soil and the noxious air, the plants inspire quantities of cadmium and lead which live in the fruit. When the news says our air quality is "unacceptable," plants have even less choice than most of us to do anything but go on breathing it. In the City, it turns out, we're forced to choose between eating the vegetables poisoned by agribusiness or the ones that have had to poison themselves.

So we didn't delve in the dirt. We didn't grow a thing.

Maybe there was no substitute for the woods.

č

The phone in his ear when should have been quiet woke him with ringing.

H'llo, he said, whuh?

Hi, how ya doin?

Who?

It was Bill the lover.

You wanna come out an have a drink, Bill said.

Are you crazy? do you know what time it is? Three, no, almost four in the morning?

Sure. I know. That's O.K. How about it?

I don't want to have a drink with you any time, man, let alone in the middle of the night.

Hey, come on, why the hell not? I think we ought to get to know each other better. After all, we do have a lot in common.

Now listen, you bastard, we don't have a goddam thing in common, so just hang up and go to sleep, willya?

Sure we do. You know. You know what we have in common.

You goddam son of a bitch, you nervy bastard, what the hell kind of a creep are you? I'm not going to talk to you about—

Writing. I meant writing. See, there you go, jumping to conclusions. Just relax man, you know? She said you were a writer.

Oh?

Yeah, sure. And there's this novel, you know, a new one I've been working on. I really need to talk about it. So

I figured you might like to come on in to the City, and we can have a drink, talk, and, like I said, get to know each other better.

O.K., pal, now look. It's four in the fucking morning and I have a nine o'clock class. I need my sleep and I don't want to know you better. I wish I didn't know you at all. You must have an agent, an editor, you've got admiring fans and reviewers, you might even have a couple of friends, though that's hard to believe. There probably are dozens of people who'd just be thrilled to death to sit through the night, bullshitting with you about Art. So leave me alone, willya, why pick on me?

You're really a very unreasonable person, you know, Bill said. Now don't get excited, and just think for a minute, you'll see. Of course I should call you. You're the one I want to talk to. We should get to know each other better.

Are you drunk? is that it? stoned, smashed, whatever? What kind of maniac are you anyway?

Why don't you come and see? You can come over here, I'll give you the address. Come on, man, what are you afraid of?

Hey, Bill said, hello? hey, are you there, hello?

Because that had stopped him. For a moment he'd considered, Was he afraid? and, What was he afraid of?

But only for a moment. Now what he felt was the insidiousness, the compelling naked will determined to have its way. And that just stoked his anger.

O.K., you bastard, he said, now listen carefully. I've had it, you hear? You don't get insulted so I can't insult you, maybe I can't get through to you at all. But just for the record, I don't want to talk to you about writing. And I'm sure as shit not going to talk to you about my wife. And whether I'm afraid, or whatever, you can think what you want, it just isn't to the point. As far as I'm concerned, day or night, you're a disaster. About the last thing I need is to get to know you better. I got enough troubles without taking your case. So, believe me, pal, you really did call the wrong guy.

He did not wait for an answer but banged down the receiver. Ten minutes later the phone rang again. He did not answer; listened for awhile, then, to its accompaniment, went and got a drink of bourbon right from the bottle, no ice, no glass. The phone stopped, but he couldn't get to sleep. And soon it rang again.

He went into the bathroom (it rang and rang) and showered until he was sure he could hear it no more.

"A few more passing suns will see us here no more and our dust and bones will mingle with these same prairies," John said. I am quoting. "I see as in a vision the dying spark of our council fires, the ashes cold and white. I see no longer the curling smoke rising from our lodge poles. I hear no longer the songs of the women as they prepare the meal. The antelope have gone; the buffalo wallows are empty; only the wail of the coyote is heard." Those are the words of Plenty Coups, John said.

He saw it, he knew what was coming. "The white man's medicine is stronger than ours." The old chiefs looked it in the face, they saw their end. Even an occasional victory couldn't change it, they knew their way was dying. But even so, they couldn't convince themselves that what would succeed them was better. The whiteman's way was stronger, of course, but they couldn't see it as better.

I can certainly feel for them, Hope said, believe me. Cause, just now, Chief, we're in their situation, even more than you. I mean us writers and talkers and teachers, the ones who value words. Here we are, still sittin around, eatin up food and breathin in the stinky air, but we're done. The future is already here, and it ain't ours. Our time is past.

It's altogether appropriate, then, said Jules, that the next President of America will be a scientist.

Jules was sure the Democrat would win this Election.

He has ties to the old America, Jules said, the Navy background, and there's the rural, farm background, the peanuts and all. That's really just business background, of course, he's no farmer, although it is true that his particular profit-product is more typical of America's past in that it really does grow in dirt. But this guy's not strictly a businessman and he's certainly no lawyer. His degree is in physics.

Then, said Anna, if the Democrat does win, the first of America's next two hundred years will be under the direction of a type not known to the two hundred before.

So that will make it very clear, I think, said Hassan, that those who say America is a country without ruins are wrong. For you, my friends, and I, too, for that matter, we will all fall upon the great heap of rubble which this nation has spent its history to erect. Not only you, John Whitlock, and your people, but your tribe as well, Hope, Jules, Anna, Ariel, and you, my friend, our tribe, too, was, as we now put it, "programmed" for extinction.

He didn't say anything.

I can understand very well, said Hassan, why you and your Thoreau would want to go to the woods, why you would turn your attention to the Indians.

He said nothing.

We knew he could speak for hours on the subject. But he didn't say a thing. We waited. We tried to let the silence bloom.

Nothing.

"A few more moons, a few more winters—and not one

of the descendants of the mighty hosts that once moved over this broad land or lived in happy homes, protected by the Great Spirit, will remain to mourn over the graves of a people once more powerful and hopeful than yours," John said. I am quoting once more, this time from Seathl. He was right—though not quite farsighted enough. A few of us are left, and we're not in the mood for mourning. Some ruins can be rebuilt, a kind of anti-urban renewal, maybe. Us red anachronisms, ugh, we find our place in present time.

I can well believe it for the Poquosset, Ariel said, and I can take heart from that, at least a little. But, is it as Hassan says? What of our tribe? What are we to do in the postliterate world where technology succeeds the text and the print-out replaces print? The chiefs you quote were great speakers. But how would we know their words if not from books? At least some of the time what they said was translated and written down. Some of us still write things down, things that won't work as well on tape or punch cards. But who is there left to read? Who cares any more for the written word?

It's true, said Hope, all true. But it lasted pretty good for awhile. Five hundred years a moveable type, that's not so bad. It's all over now or soon, but in those five hundred years Europe and America learned to read, and Dickens drew em in like the Beatles.

I remember them, said Hassan, the Beatles, yes. But, you know, if what you say is true, what is to become of my people who have not yet learned to read? Whoever you elect as your President will be glad to sell my people's flesh and soul for oil. Your Election will not alter the fact that my people will not even have the chance to learn to read. They will skip your five hundred years of printed words and go from the ancient illiteracy to the modern illiteracy. In just a little time they also will stare upon the blank flicker of the television screen. It will be the only light shining as they come out of the darkness. They will never read with care and passion. What sight they attain will be only shadowsight, not insight, never the light inside the mind, the first flame of understanding.

We were silent for a moment.

Then Jules said, Of course there's a certain loss, no doubt about it, and O.K., there's real danger, too. But think of the possibilities. Let's not just be sentimental about the past.

Come on, Jules, Hope said, you know I'm not. I'm plenty realistic about the bad old days and I've tried to live as if there's a future. I think. I think, for instance, about the kids, ya know? How about them, these new land pioneers, this bunch a foresters without trees? I see them shoulderin their little calculators and headin out to make settlements in this brave new world. But I worry for em, Jules, ya know? And I bet you do too. What, Jules, what do they know, these cute little Americans? what will they know?

Yes, yes, exactly, said Hassan. I must shudder for your American children as I shudder for mine. For that matter, if they can remain unharmed, my children will be American children, I suppose. And what is that to be? I look around, and I very nearly can understand, that one might really as a matter of principle choose to remain childless out of horror, in revulsion against the world to come.

It is not easy to be encouraged, Anna said, to think of a world that cannot read, a world that is already here. My son finds himself at odds with many his age. It's fortunate he is so fond of sports, otherwise his passion for reading could get him into trouble. But still, if we vote at all, I think our vote will have to be for the Scientist candidate. The other is quite impossible.

And that brings me back to the subject of our Centennial Celebration, the Chief said, and to Mr. General Custer.

How so, we said.

You remember I told you that Custer might have been President if not for the intervention of us Indians?

We remembered.

Well, the Little Big Horn Fight didn't forestall our deaths at Wounded Knee and the long death after. But at least it did keep Pahuska out of the White House. So there you have it, a hundred years after your tea party at Boston, the Indian is again at the center of America's history. On the eve of your first Centennial Celebration, we influenced your choice of President. And, maybe more important, until the North Vietnamese did it, we handed the Army its biggest defeat by guerrilla fighters. The Little Big Horn, it was the last great victory of the non-technologists.

č

His wife said, Well, I hear you and Bill had quite a little party together.

What do you mean, he said, I don't understand.

Oh, come on now, you know, he told me. You went out drinking together. Really got down, that's what he said. He said you two really understood each other now.

Oh, he said.

Then he told her the truth.

She started to cry.

He had seen her cry a lot lately.

Still, he did not say what came fast to his lips. He made his hand not reach to touch.

He sat like a lump and watched her cry.

I'm sorry, she said, my nerves are bad.

Look, he said, forget it. I mean, don't apologize, there's

no need. But, also, if there's anything I can do, I mean anything you think I could do, well, I'd like to do it.

I think the kids miss you.

I miss them, too. Noise and all. Fussing, whining, all of it.

You can't miss the fussing. Ten minutes of it, you know, you wouldn't miss it. Hey, is it all right with you and—really, I forget her name, the Indian woman?

Sure, he said, why not. Just fine. Only I haven't seen her for awhile. They've been busy, her friends and all. They've been working on this Centennial thing, I think I mentioned it, a kind of counter-Bicentennial. They should have a mailing going out pretty soon. And there's been a lot to take care of about getting the land back. Even with my signing it over to them, there's still plenty to worry about. So I really haven't seen much of her. Look, I don't even know why she bothered with me. I mean, it was good for awhile, but—Anyway, you know, I don't do so well alone.

And the gangsters? what's with them?

I don't know, nothing, I guess. Why, have you heard anything?

No, no, nothing. I just wondered.

Well, I think there's nothing to do about them except what Jules says, just to try to forget them and to believe they're done with us. If they still want that land, they'll have to try and get it through the courts. Why, have the kids said anything? Has it been bothering them, what happened?

But she was crying again.

What? he said, what is it? Have the kids had nightmares or something?

It wasn't anything like that.

There's not too much furniture in here, is there? she said. I mean, look, there isn't really much at all.

No, he said, of course not, but—

He says he gets headaches from it, it's so cluttered. Bill says he can't even breathe in here, it's so crowded with furniture and junk.

Oh, he said. He gets headaches.

He stood up to go.

I tell you, he said, all he means is it's finally got through to him. Real people take up space. And any kid's a crowd.

ċ

You've packed a few things?

Yes.

Good. Then we are ready.

Now then, we must first check the car carefully. Look around please, will you? Underneath, too? Fine, just trust to your instinct. Does everything seem all right? You have no sense of something not quite as usual? It does not matter that you see nothing, you will be able to sense something like that. Under the bonnet, now, please, my friend. Raise it carefully, slowly. Good. Now, how does it seem to you?

Fine, there's nothing wrong that I can tell.

Excellent, my friend. We will now try the doors. Carefully, again, and slowly. No, don't sit down as yet. Have a look under the seats. And the glove box? Everything is all right? Can you think of some place else we might want to check? No? So, very well. I think then we may start.

He put the key into the ignition very gingerly and did not allow himself even to breathe as he turned it. The engine caught and he found himself smiling broadly at Hassan.

Hassan smiled broadly back.

O.K., he said, where are we going?

Just now, first to the Holland Tunnel. And then I think we shall try a bit of the New Jersey Turnpike. We have many choices of route. You will see. I will direct you.

As he drove the station wagon across town and then turned South to the Tunnel, he found himself constantly checking the rear view mirror. Were they being followed? Could he "make" a "tail?" He realized he knew nothing of such things other than what he saw on the tv which lied.

I guess it's like what Jules always tells us, he said, I guess they really are out there, the bad guys.

He thought of Peter and noticed now the white scar just below Hassan's hairline. He checked again the mirror to the back.

I can understand it now, I can really see, he said, how it's not paranoid to be careful. It's only sensible.

He tried to smile.

Hassan nodded. He did not smile back.

The Tall Ships were coming!

Foretold by the news voice, the Tall Ships soon were hailed by every voice with joyful anticipation. Promised for this Glorious Fourth was a fleet of the world's great sailing ships in progress down our Lordly Hudson. The water, the wind, the broad sails: these would help to set our minds on freedom.

Except that Chile's blood boat, the *Esmeralda*, was to be among them. We thought that this was wrong, for what we'd learned of her, although the news voice did not speak of it, made it unfit that she participate in an anniversary of Independence.

When our CIA overthrew the legitimately elected government of Chile, those it put in charge soon ran out of room to torture the many who remained in opposition to the coup. They crowded all the prisons, they filled the basement offices and empty rooms of barracks, and still there wasn't space enough to deal with those who would not say Yes or might say No.

And so, in a burst of creative intelligence worthy of the Central Intelligence, their sponsor, the Generals enlisted Sport on behalf of the Nation. Chile's soccer stadia were brought into use as detention and interrogation centers, and her white jewel of the sea, the beautiful *Esmeralda*, entered the service of pain. The tall ship's decks ran red with blood, with muck beyond the stock of veins and arteries, while from below decks rang cries and shrieks wilder than the seabirds' circling overhead.

The *Esmeralda* was a beautiful boat (for we'd seen pictures), but we couldn't accept its presence as appropriate to a celebration of liberty and justice for all. None of Her unwilling guests had returned to shore after just one quiet night.

And so we wrote letters and sent petitions to our Government. We requested respectfully and angrily demanded. To no avail. The under-aides who answered said, Don't spoil the show. We were assured the *Esmeralda*'s decks had been wellscrubbed. No reason to fuss, what did it matter. No one really cared, anyway. Why couldn't we for once just let be and go along?

Instructed by our absent friend, we thought of Thoreau approaching like ourselves another Fourth of July and troubled by his country's actions. Massachusetts had returned the innocent black man Anthony Burns to slavery and Thoreau was "surprised to see men going about their business as if nothing had happened." We were almost past surprising, and even tried ourselves to go about our business as if nothing had happened.

But whatever it took, we didn't have it. "Who can be serene," we wondered with Thoreau, "in a country where both the rulers and the ruled are without principle?"

Lots of people, obviously. But we couldn't. And we really had tried.

č

Miles on the Jersey, then on to the Pennsylvania Turnpike, South. Then they got off the big road; got back on again. Now north.

The rearward mirror showed flux and change, the nothing special he wanted to see.

Exited north, back on to the Pennsylvania Pike, repeating south for awhile until Hassan said, Take the exit for Route —.

They went along and they went along, made a turn, turned again. And passing through a most ordinary little town, Hassan said, There, pull up just there and park.

They got out and walked the remainder of the way, around and around some corners, up and back several blocks. Then Hassan stopped.

All right, my friend, Hassan said, thank you for your patience. Here we are at last. This house is our destination.

Before they knocked the door was opened to them. In the doorway, a whitehaired woman with clear clear blue eyes said, Welcome. Then she stood aside to let them in.

A car pulled up to the curb. Behind the wheel a whitehaired man with double clear blue eyes. He smiled and waved.

God bless you, said the woman. We'll be back on Sunday night. You know where to reach us if need be.

She joined her husband in the car and the two drove off.

Quakers, he said.

Why, yes, said Hassan. He closed the door behind them

and locked it carefully. You're right, but how did you know?

He started to say when down the stairs came hurtling two small sons. A dark woman motherlike followed, trying to hold in their neckbreak speed.

Aha! said Hassan, as he bent to catch his flying boys, now you see where we are and whom we have come to visit!

Burdened with boys, Hassan found also in his arms now room to gather his wife.

The father and children, husband and wife, laughed and cried, falling into chairs and also out, the father and the sons rolling wildly on the rug, hugs and kisses, kisses and hugs all around. Then back into chairs out of which all talked fast flinging words of Persian everywhere at once.

He made a place for himself in the corner of the room. He sat, he watched, waiting, waiting, he listened.

And though there was not a single known word of that foreign language in his head, he understood what they said most perfectly.

Jules opened the door and it was Joey.

Oh, said Jules, it's you. Who's with you?

Whathehell ya mean, who's with me? Me, just me, that's who, Joey said. Waddaya think, huh? That time you come aroun to see me, makin out like ya know things I don't even know, did I ask who was with you, did I? So what is this here, who's with me? You gonna let me in or what?

Yeah, sure, come in, come in, Jules said. But he's not here now.

I know he ain't here, Joey said, he went off with that Ay-rab guy. That's why I come jus now, cause he ain't here. I figgered he wouldn't wanna see me. But I thought, you people are his friends an all, maybe you'd hear me out. Cause I still feel bad on account a what happened. Not that I know who snatched his kids, but like I tol ya, I got kids too an I can unnerstan what it is, somethin like that happens to a guy. So me, an Tony,—Tony, too. He feels bad, too—

Well, ya oughta feel bad, ya bum ya, said Hope, pickin on kids like that, ya bum.

Hey, hey, said Joey, what's goin on here? Who's the crazy ol broad?

And who are you, said Anna, who's the fat old fart?

Hope, Anna, please, said Ariel, Jules, come on now, all of you. Mr. Coniglio, it's such a lovely day, how about it if we all go outside? Maybe we could talk better there.

Geez, thanks, lady, sure. I mean, a guy takes his life in

his hands comin to see you people! Sure, let's go outside. I can't hear a goddam thing anyhow with that radio goin like that.

We walked out to Tompkins Square Park.

There was a big scene in Jules's best novel set in this Park, and Hope, whose field lay further West, also had written several Park stories. In one of them the main character stays up in a tree almost the whole time. We could imagine why to look around, for in the trees green was victor and spring in gaudy occupation. On the ground in motion were legs and arms and hair again, not wool and suede and a tassel on top.

We sat in line on a bench. Joey cleared his throat. We listened hard.

I come, he said, to make amens. Yer friend the perfesser, he's a nut. No offense, but I think all a you people are nuts. But still, I like the guy, really, I do, an I'm sorry for all the grief he been through. So what I done, I wrote this here letter, and I thought, since you're his friends, if ya'd take a look at it, an make corrections, ya know, on anythin I ain't said right, I can give it to Tina who does the books, an get it all typed up nice. Then I'll send it to the perfesser, an that's it, finished, g'bye. With the land up there, whatever's gonna be, mostly it's gonna be up to the courts, ya know, nothin personal. So anyway, that's why I come.

He handed over an envelope. We read the letter inside.

Hope said, Listen Joey, just like it is, it's good like that, leave it like it is.

It's fine, Ariel said, really. It says everything.

Hey, Joey said, you ain't, waddaya call it, patronizin me or somethin, ya ain't puttin me on or nothin?

No, no, said Anna, of course not, not at all. I agree with Ariel and Hope, and—Jules, don't you think so, too? What you say here is fine just as it is. There's nothing you need to change.

Ya think he'll unnerstan how I'm not on'y just *sayin* I'm sorry how things turned out? Cause, ya know, talk is cheap. But I want he should know I went an done somethin, I done it with my own two hands, up there, in the woods. I ain't tellin him what to do, but if he wants, he can go up there an see for himself, he can see with his own eyes what I done to make amens.

We must again examine the car, I think, just as before we did. Better to be safe. And then we will go home.

They lifted the hood and opened the doors and hit their knees to look well underneath.

The car was all right and now they drove direct. He still checked the mirror to the rear and still it was innocent in reflection.

Why did you take me along, Hassan? he said. How come you asked me to drive you?

Hassan laughed. How did you know our hosts were Quakers?

A lot of things, I guess. I could probably make a list of the traits. But, finally, that wouldn't explain it. I just knew, that's all.

Exactly, said Hassan. I also.

❧

I want to go to the woods, he said.

Sure, she said, whatever. Do what you want.

No, I mean, I wanted—I was wondering if, you know, maybe if, just to see it once, if you might come along.

She paused.

I might, she said. Only, you know, maybe not yet.

How about the kids, he said, do you think they would want to come?

Sure, I think so. You have to ask them. It's fine with me.

She had a bruise on her cheek. It was a goodbye present from Bill. He felt sorry for her. For himself he felt glad.

It was nice to have visible confirmation that someone you hated was hateworthy.

Even with the bruise she looked better. Goodbye Bill. Anything might happen now.

How about a drive to the country, kids, he said.

Yay yay, goody, said his girl.

Boo, boring, said the boy. You said we could go to the zoo, you promised.

He argued a little, then gave in. It was a nice day for animals too.

How about next Sunday, he said.

No, today, said the girl. If we can't go today, I won't go next Sunday.

Yay, yay, said the boy.

Have fun at the zoo, said his wife.

He took the kids and off they went.

When he got Joey's letter he phoned his wife.

I especially want to take the kids up to the woods on

Sunday, he said. If it seems O.K., could you talk it up?
Because I just got this letter from Joey Coniglio, and—

Oh, my god, she said.

No, no, hey, listen, don't worry. Really, it's O.K. He's
very apologetic, and he writes he's done something up
there to make amends. So I figured I ought to go see.
I'd like the kids to come too. I'm sure it'll be all right.

When he asked us to go to the woods we said, All right. He asked if John could meet us, and also Fawn Coat and Maria. April rain or sunshine, next Sunday we would gather in the woods he had wanted, the woods the Poquosset might have forever.

The station wagon led the way up the Palisades, to 9W, 52, then 208 into Walden. Walden, N.Y. Most of the way the kids were good and when restless quieted down for the extraordinary animal sounds Hassan could make. Roosters crowing and asses braying were kinder on the driver's nerves than the sounds of two kids fighting.

The rest of us followed in Hope's VW bus. And soon we saw the Wallkill River, full of melt and rain. And then the clearing that once was his woods.

John's pickup was already there. We saw the Chief himself, Fawn Coat, and Maria, stretched out on the new grass.

We got out and hugged all around—then backed off and laughed.

I wondered when you sleepyheads would get here, John said, it's after twelve. He went to a cooler in the pickup for cans of beer which he tossed to one and all. Cokes for the thirsty kids.

Ariel took out a smoke. Our friend struck the match that gave her a light.

This is great, said Jules, now if Hope will only tell me where the hell the sandwiches are.

I saw you looking for em while I was driving, Hope said, you Marxists and your appetite! Here, here you go.

I want tuna fish, said his boy.

Yuk, cheese for me, said his girl, yum.

Tuna is yum, the boy said.

All right, all right, he said. His wife was right. This part was hard to miss. Though not so hard to take.

So, he said, here we are.

There we were.

What also was, we saw, was two newplanted pines where once had been two bigger trees. Those had borne signs reading

PROPERTY OF

CONIGLIO BROS., INC.

and

PROPERTY OF

THE POQUOSSET TRIBE

but these were unencumbered.

Do you think this is what Joey meant, he said.

There seemed no way to doubt. These two young pines were Joey's amens.

They had been planted with care. The dirt around the roots was tamped down hard, and—whether from recent rain or human help—nice and moist. Treetape was wrapped around the base of each. And he explained to the kids what that was for, to protect the tender bark from animals or accident.

They seemed impressed. Then set out to explore. Don't go too far, he said.

John said, Once a long time ago, the Great Spirit asked all the trees to watch and keep awake. They did their best, but after awhile, the great oaks and maples, the tall locust and hickory, the choke-cherries and elms all fell asleep. Only the fir and hemlock and cedar, and the great-great-grandparents of these pines stayed up as they had been asked. And they were rewarded with the privilege of keeping green all through the year, winter as well as summer.

So I'm really happy to see these new trees. It will be good here in these woods of mostly sleepy trees to have some watchful evergreens. When the title to this land is clear and my people come here to live, I promise you these pines won't be disturbed.

There's something else I want to tell you and I guess this is as good a time as any, while I've got the floor. We hope you'll let us adopt you as a Poquosset. You see, in the old days, when hard winters, sickness, or warfare depleted the tribe, friendly strangers or captives of war were adopted into individual families as sons or daughters, sisters and brothers, husbands and wives. They filled out our numbers and lived among us as equals, the same as if they had been born Poquosset.

If that sounds odd to you, or like more than you ever had in mind, let me say a word about the tradition regarding friends and guests. A friend of the Poquosset, even not one of the tribe, can visit whenever he wants and stay as long as he wants. And that's not just empty rhetoric, it's for real. A day, a month, whatever, someone we know and welcome is someone for whom we're glad to accept responsibility. I've talked all of this over with my parents and sister, with Nelson and Tim and Maria, with all the Poquosset. And we're in agreement. When it comes to the land, property rights are a white man's notion mostly, enforced on these shores by Puritans and businessmen. For Indians what prevailed was more nearly what your courts call usufruct, the right of use. To help us, you've given up your right of property. I want to tell you on behalf of all the Poquosset that there's no way you can give up your right of use to this land in our eyes. These woods don't belong to any of us to own and keep. But I hope they'll be for us and you to use.

So tell your kids they can be Indians if they want and have some funny names. Or you can just come stay with us whenever you like.

č

Henry David Thoreau died on the 6th of May, 1862, with his mother and sisters around him, still the wifeless woodsman.

In the last weeks of his life Thoreau worried for the Country he'd so often opposed and always loved. Earlier in the year Fort Sumter had been fired upon and the North had declared war. Lincoln, whom he trusted far less than he'd trusted John Brown, was President. He told his sisters he could never get well until the War was over. He was right. His birthday, like America's, was in July, but he didn't live to celebrate. The War went on. Thoreau died.

Ever the spokesman for beginnings, a man who'd had his troubles with the middle of life, Thoreau was in fine form as he approached the end. His Aunt Louisa asked him if he'd made his peace with God and he told her, "I did not know we had ever quarrelled." A friend inquired

whether Thoreau could now see The Opposite Shore, and
he was advised, "One world at a time." Sam Staples who
had been his jailer for a night in 1845 came to visit and
left reporting that he'd never spent an hour with more
satisfaction.

Henry Thoreau had done his best to change this one world
for a long time, living with it and often against it, but
always firmly in it (no blithe spirits flew over Thoreau's
head; his ducks quacked); his quarrel hadn't been with
god but with men and their institutions. And now that
his time came to change worlds, he could approve. He
thought this time he could say Yes with no loss of honor.

His good friend Channing found it hard to accept and
spoke of his sense of impending loss. But Thoreau said
simply, "It is better some things should end."

And came the morning when he was heard to say first
Moose, then Indian. And then he died.

He died and he was buried on a wooded knoll in Sleepy
Hollow Cemetery. He died—but as he'd once said of
John Brown, as Seathl had said of his people, some things
that end just don't ever die.

For us, as for our friend, Thoreau, like the Indians, lived
on.

It seemed therefore no more than proper that we gather
together on the anniversary of Thoreau's death to welcome in the spring of this year and to remember the

spring of another year. And so we planned a party for the 6th of May, 1976.

č

Hope came in a new dress and Jules wore a tie. Parts of it lighted up when he squeezed a rubber bulb in his pocket.

It's the only one I have, Jules said. Actually, I do have one other one. But I thought somebody should be the life of the party.

Tim Running entered hard, braids and fringes flying. Long time no see, *kemo sabe*, he said, Ugh! how! and all that shit. Show me the fire water, man, I feel like one bad injun.

Actually, said Nelson Running, shaking hands all around, my badass brother drinks only straight wood alcohol poured over rusty nails. Stir it with a rattlesnake, if you've got one handy.

What a coincidence, Fawn Coat said, that's just how I take mine.

Can I interest no one in my humble mint tea? said Hassan. It's really quite good.

Or a toke off this joint, Maria said, it's healthier than alcohol and less fattening.

If we were doing things right, he said, what we'd be drinking would be water. That was Thoreau's drink.

We agreed. No one switched.

The bell rang and Anna opened. He stepped forward.

I didn't know if you'd come, he said.

You didn't exactly invite me either, his wife said.

Well, I did, he said, sort of I did. I got scared. But I guess you could figure out when and where. Here you are.

Here I am.

Uh, right. How are the kids?

They're spending the night at my mother's, I—Oh, *how* are they, you said. They're fine, great. They said they had a terrific time with you and your friends up in the woods. It sounds nice up there, really. I'd like to see it some time. And the kids, they're almost ready to go live up there.

Don't worry about that, he said. There's no danger of that, that part's all over.

Hey, said John Whitlock Chief of the Poquosset, I heard that. And at the risk of sticking my nose in where angels fear to tread, let me remind you of what I said before. The Lone Ranger and his family are welcome any time on the lands of the Poquosset, as friends, or if you want, as relatives, any time and forever, to visit or to live. But wait a minute, I don't think I've been introduced to this lovely lady here.

Me neither, said Maria.

Or me, said Fawn Coat.

Nelson and Tim also joined them. So, in a minute, awkwardly with smiles, he'd introduced his wife to all the Poquosset, his friends.

A silence broken by the bell; we opened and found who we were missing, Ariel.

I'm sorry, she said, I know I'm late. I was working on a poem. I'd had a hard time with it for so long, I figured while it was going all right I'd better stay with it until I finished or had to quit.

We noticed Ariel's hair was different.

Oh, she said, sure, didn't you know? I used to rinse it dark. It's been full of gray for years.

We didn't know. Never even suspected.

Anna said, You look wonderful. Now you really look like yourself.

All right, said Jules, but tell us, what happened?

I don't know, said Ariel, I'm not sure. Let me read you some of what I've got, O.K.?

> . . . *the fire*
> *died down in the open ground*
>
> *and they made a place for themselves.*
> *It wasn't much good,*
> *they'd fall, and freeze,*
>
> *some of them said*
> *Well, it was all they could,*
>
> *some said it was beautiful, some days,*
> *the way the little ones took to the water,*
> *and some lay smoking, smoking,*
>
> *and some burned up for good,*
> *and some waited,*
> *lasting, staring*
> *over each other's merciful shoulders. . . .*

I wanted to be able to bring that much of it tonight, you know, for all of you, for Thoreau, and for the Indians.

We thanked her. Some kissed.

Then we drifted off one way and another, in search of food or drink—tea and wine, and bourbon without ice— or pungent pot, in search of one thing or another.

Anna said, No, I'd rather not, really, no. But then at Hope's urging, we heard her beautiful low voice reciting slowly in German.

Tim and the Chief with gestures were telling a joke to
Jules who chewed like mad to beat the punch line.

Ariel stood alone, puffing on a cigarette, staring at the
wall or the smoke that climbed and climbed upward.

In the other room the radio was off. We'd pulled the plug.
There was no news we needed. For the present, we
wanted to think a little of the past. Of the past, and the
future, at least for the Indians and maybe for our friend.

He sat with his wife in a corner of the room, talking
talking, their faces almost touching, not looking around
or away. The kids were at her mother's for the night.
Anything might happen.

And we were happy for a moment, talking, drinking, eating, smoking, laughing.

Ariel's poem would one day find its closing lines to put
in words not how it really was at all but how it felt,
when, though only for a moment, we'd

> *known always*
> *whispering*
> *Why are we in this life.*

New York, 1978
For Cynthia, Tanya, and Jeremy